❦❦❦❦❦❦❦❦ FLIGHT OF WHITE CROWS

By John Berry

Krishna Fluting
Flight of White Crows
Stories, Tales, and Paradoxes

Flight of White Crows

Stories, Tales, and Paradoxes

JOHN BERRY

New York — The Macmillan Company — 1961

First Printing

Thanks are due to the magazines in which the following stories first appeared: to *Western Review* for "The Sermon of the Flies" and "Jawaharlal and the Three Cadavers"; to *Antioch Review* for "The Golden Hair"; to the *Southwest Review* for "Beyond Ganga Mata"; to *Harper's Magazine* for "The Touchable"; to *New World Writing* for "The Listener"; to *The Magazine of Fantasy and Science Fiction* for "The One Who Returns"; to *Virginia Quarterly Review* for "The Lamp from Tarok Dzong"; to *Contact* for "The Sibling"; and to *The Noble Savage* for "Flight of White Crows." Some of the stories have been revised for this collection.

More than thanks are due to the beautiful and constant ones—Hattie, Ynez, Eliena—who helped me to survive, to live, to write whatever is contained in this book.—J. B.

Printed in the United States of America

The Macmillan Company, New York
Brett-Macmillan Ltd., Galt, Ontario

Library of Congress catalog card number: 61-13521

to my wife

I used to think that my habit of self-plagiarism (phrases, passages, and people have emigrated out of these stories into the open spaces of a novel, *Krishna Fluting,* and one or two malcontents seem to have applied for a return visa) arose from a lack of inventiveness. That was a lazy explanation. I now incline to the belief that these repeatings are the result of an unwillingness to tamper with first manifestations, because in my mind the particular reality is inseparable from the particular vehicle, which may take the form of a recurrent dream, day or night, with or without words. Against the charge of being slightly obsessed with these particulars, I am defenseless. It may be that they have not finished with me even yet.

CONTENTS

EIGHT STORIES

THREE TALES

THE PIOUS PUZZLES OF
ANANDA MAHADEV

EIGHT STORIES

The Golden Hair

"Myth embodies the nearest approach to absolute truth that can be stated in words."
—A. K. COOMARASWAMY

Sooner or later, people ask me why I went to India, and this is a delicate question requiring a different answer each time, not because I must conceal the truth, but because the truth seems different to me every time I think seriously about it. Every new experience affects the meaning of the whole past; and if we agree that this is so, we can add to our worries the thought that not even the coffined past holds still—or we can smile with the Buddha by the River of Life, in that philosophical calm which comes from knowledge of the unity and the transitoriness of all things.

For some reason no one has ever asked me why I *left* India. Say I went there to study Myth, or to find out what was on the other side of the moon, or to see what the world looks like from Mars; say I was escaping from something or pursuing something— love, perhaps. It is all true. And if I say that I was nearly lost there, and that I was pulled out by a hair—a golden one—you will understand that it is true; and yet the very strangeness of it is enough to assure me that I shall probably, in all honesty, tell my story a bit differently next time. I am too much concerned with a sense of proportion in this life, ever to be satisfied with facts.

At any rate, I went to India and I stayed there for three years— which, in a land where time has no meaning, can be a moment or a lifetime. In my case it was almost a lifetime. Bharat University, at Bharatpur, where I settled in October, 1951, is a hundred miles inland from Calcutta, in Bengal, near the Behar border, and it is surrounded by desert and jungle. It used to be an *ashram*, or hermitage. Now it is a school, with primary, secondary, college and postgraduate departments. Total enrollment is about five hundred, mostly high-caste Bengalis, with quite a few students from other provinces. Foreigners come there from time to time, with the idea of teaching the texts of modern knowledge or studying the texts of ancient wisdom. I did both, with unflagging folly.

The community, clustered loosely around the school, is composed of Bengali families connected in one way or another with the institution. For various reasons—the inferior status of women in India, Bengali apartheid, religious and caste restrictions and the prohibitive cost of Indian hospitality—social life is at a standstill. As a foreigner, and not a very aggressive one at that, I found myself shut out of Bengali life, although I adopted Indian dress, lived in a mud hut, spoke Bengali, and devoted myself to friendship as if I thought the world depended on it—and, as a matter of fact, I did think so. Only Arjuna babu, the local chief of police, who had spent ten years in the British Army of the Middle East, was sufficiently disoriented as to require perspectives outside the culture of Bengal. To this day he is my loyal and solitary Indian friend; but I never saw his family. Finally, there was Balu, my cook, a bowlegged little rogue of a Sudra—that is, a member of the servant caste—who was an insufferable snob because some people had seen fit to be half a degree blacker than he, and that was black indeed. Balu was pious, immoral, and dishonest as the day is long, but I loved him because he was jolly and a good flutist. Once, in a fit of despondency, I actually began negotiating to buy my way into his home for a social evening. We were both relieved when events made this particular prostitution unnecessary.

Bharatpur is a kind of "Aryan" colony in the midst of Dravidian territory. That is, the surrounding people are the black tribesmen whose ancestors inhabited the land when the fair ancestors of present-day Brahmans and Kshatriyas, the Aryans, came down from the north and conquered India. It was among these people, the Santals, whom other Indians call "aborigines" and "non-Indians," that I found friendship and true hospitality in that complex, subtle, and hidebound land for which I bear a nearly unrequited love.

My mud hut—to me, the most beautiful of houses—was simply alive with creatures. There were no parasites except mosquitoes, but there must have been thirty different kinds of insects, of which the two-inch cockroaches were the most scholarly and intelligent. Myna birds, with delicious little chuckles, searched the thatched roof for crawling tidbits. At night two cobras came to drink at the leaky water tank just outside. Tiny bats fluttered in and out of my windows. From three to seven *tik-tikis*—lizards of various shades of green or gray—took up their station every night on the wall, not two feet from my chair, where they caught the insects that were attracted by my reading lamp; and one of these lizards sometimes closed her eyes and allowed me to stroke her head with my forefinger. Scorpions as big as my hand and centipedes as long as my foot sometimes made dramatic entrances and quick exits. For a whole summer month two extraordinarily handsome but churlish storks woke me at six o'clock every morning by pounding on the veranda, clapping their beaks and, I think, growling. They liked bread, but they also liked to tower over me suddenly with a mad look in their eyes. My defense was to throw a cloth over their heads when they did this. (An incautious Bengali woman had to have her head stitched up after a meeting with these cantankerous birds.) And there were all manner of smaller birds, and there were monkeys and apes and jackals and dogs and mice and ants. . . .

There was no question of getting rid of all these creatures. I had to live with them, and on the whole they were pretty well behaved. After all, they had to live somewhere. Few of them had any specific designs on my person. Mosquitoes were fascinated by my pale, succulent feet, and if they encountered insect repellent on them, they went away and sat down and thought. On the average, two flies out of twelve were curious. These I swatted, and the rest could stay. Gloomily I felled an occasional great beetle merely because he crashed into my hut like an airplane and roared and thudded around; besides, he carried a lot of little fuzzy yellow passengers underneath, who scattered when he hit. Finally, there were the rats, with whom I declined to share my living quarters. They were shameless fellows with no poise and they made me damned nervous. I murdered them with a stick.

One morning I was walking away from my hut carrying a dead rat by the tail, when a young Santal tribesman darted away from his companions on the road nearby, and came running toward me. He was naked except for a minim breechclout, a red *gamcha*, or sweatcloth, around his head, a blue-and-white necklace, and copper amulets worn around the neck and just above the elbows. His lithe black body glistened with coconut oil. A bamboo bow and reed arrows were slung across his back. As he approached, he slowed to a walk, flashed the pearliest of smiles, and clasped his hands in the *namaskar*, sign of greeting.

"Babu," he said, "what will you do with the rat?"

"Bury it," I replied. I noticed that his Bengali was elementary, like mine, and I was delighted that he did not call me Sahib.

"Give it to me."

"And what will you do with it?"

"Eat it." He grinned, and, taking the rat, saluted me with it and flew off to rejoin his fellows.

The next morning, with a green shawl over his shoulders, he was back at my hut, dragging a huge dead fruit bat, or flying fox, by the wingtip. It was about as big as a California buzzard. With an expression of pure happiness, he dropped the creature at my door and started off.

"Just a minute, friend," I called. "What is this for?"

"Eat it. I shot it last night. My father sends it to you."

"What do these bats eat?" I had a fleeting vision of a bat roasted with a mouse in its mouth. At this point almost anything would have been preferable to goat, which had been my only meat for many months. Had any other meat been available, Balu would have refused to cook it for me. Good Hindu that he was, he lived in dread that I—and perhaps he unknowingly!—might commit the abomination of eating "beeph." Even now he was peeking through the window, rolling his eyes and wagging his head at Sahib's dubious association with a savage and a bat.

"They eat only the best of mangoes," the Santal assured me. "We eat only the best of bats."

"How do you cook them?"

He became pensive.

"I do not know," he said at last. "My mother and my sisters know. Will you eat with us—or are you a Brahman?"

"I am not even a Hindu," I said.

He slapped his chest and spun around twice, like a dancer.

"Neither are we!" he shouted. "Muslim? No! Then you are like us—only you are white." Solemnly gazing into my blue eyes, he reached out and tickled my cheek with his fingers; and, as I smiled and did the same to him, he said, "You are really like us."

Shukdev was his name. It means Happy God.

That afternoon I did not go cycling with Arjuna babu as usual. Instead I left early, avoiding the police station where he ruled over his sixteen barefoot policemen, and cycled out about five miles, across a desert, to a jungle where Shukdev had said his village was. As I walked along the trail, pushing my cycle tortuously under banyan roots and creepers, I came upon a mud hut with smoke curling up from a hole in the thatch. In front of it, gazing at me with an expression of amazement and something like joy, stood Adam, in Adam's state. And how like Shukdev he was! Short, black, perfectly proportioned, with great, liquid eyes and straight hair that hung nearly to his shoulders, he seemed to me of the same consistency throughout, balanced and harmonious with himself and his environment. And he was greeting me with that calm courtesy and grace which befits the lord of creation.

"Do you know Shukdev?" I asked.

"He is my *bhai*." This could mean brother, or a more distant relative, or a close friend. "You are the friend of Shukdev? I am Buden. I will take you to him."

Buden led me along a trail. Small razorbacked pigs scurried in front of us. Gaudy parrots screamed at us from the orchid-covered trees and vines overhead. Suddenly we were in a clearing, with a cluster of huts about us. Although, as I learned later, I was the first white man who had ever come to their village, the people of the tribe neither hid themselves nor swarmed about me. Discreet yet friendly, they stood chatting with one another. Whenever they caught me looking at them, they smiled at me encouragingly. They closely resembled Buden and Shukdev; for they were a type, formed by unchanging millenniums in the same environment: not individuated but standard. And what a standard! I thought them the most beautiful people I had ever seen.

Out of the largest hut in the village Shukdev came running to greet me, followed by a dignified older man, a middle-aged woman, and four girls—his father, mother, and sisters. After his father, Shurja, who was the chief, had welcomed me, the elders, including two matriarchal women, gathered around to exchange pleasantries. Then the festivities began. First a huge black caldron was uncovered and its steaming contents ladled out in coconut shells. I received the first cup of scalding liquid and downed it with a flourish. It was mostly fermented rice, whitish in color, and it tasted like a mixture of beer and sauterne with salt, spices, and chili added. It was extremely potent.

A humming, musical sound arose from somewhere—three notes only, repeated over and over, with subtle variations in order, rhythm, and tempo. A group of young women, their arms linked, were singing in unison, their lips barely moving, like ventriloquists. Red hibiscus flowers were in their blue-black hair, and they wore single garments like short saris—blue and green and blue-green and violet—draped so as to leave one magnificent breast more or less bare. Other girls joined them. Flutes began, then drums, lazy and eccentric to my ears, but not to theirs. The beauties lined up, arm in arm, swaying and nodding, with little shuffling complicated steps. It was like fields of rice moving in the wind.

Inside the chief's hut I sat on a mat, surrounded by Shukdev, Buden, Shurja, and Shurja's father, father-in-law, and two uncles. The women brought in earthenware bowls full of steaming rice, curried vegetables, salt and chilis, and we fell to with our fingers. There followed roast bat and curried bat, chicken and pig. There were other things which I could not identify. If there was rat, I ate it gratefully.

It was dark outside now, but two big bonfires made centers around which two groups of dancers were swaying and leaping—for the men had joined in, some with drums dangling from their necks to their waists, dancing and drumming at the same time: hopping and strutting like cocks, then beautifully with agile and very difficult steps, hovering low, soaring high, always perilously close to the semicircle of women, to whose movements theirs were in such contrast, and drumming madly with a rhythm I could never catch. Variations on the heartbeat, I thought. Shukdev and Buden, both as drunk as I and as everyone else, took my hands and showed me the steps. It was really a kind of courtship dance, the men boasting of their prowess in hunting and working, dancing, drinking, and sex—and we had to make all the appropriate noises—the women remaining almost but not quite unmoved, sensual and enigmatic.

I slept that night in the village, which is called Flower Town.

My commitments at the so noncommittal university became more and more irksome as my visits to Flower Town grew longer and more frequent. One day the acting vice chancellor indicated to me that my association with the Santals was an implied rebuke to the Hindu community—by which, of course, he meant the touch-me-not Brahmans. I told him, in effect, that I took my friendship where I found it and that I should welcome hospitality from all segments of the population, including the untouchables.

"You mean, spiritually," he said.

"No," I said, "physically. People ought to *touch* each other." And reaching out—my mind being elsewhere—I tickled his cheek ever so politely. He flinched.

Not long after that, I was relieved of my classes. And it was indeed a relief, not only because I had been unable to adjust myself to the top-heavy examination system, but because it was a small university, split into warring factions, including communists and nationalists, all of whom were pretty well agreed that I was up to no good. The fact that my best friend, Arjuna babu (that elegant and poetic Brahman, who hates and fears firearms), was the local chief of police, showed that American imperialists were busy undermining officialdom. The boxes of used clothing which I received periodically from America—for which I exploited my friends and my family—were for the purpose of influencing the loyalty of the poor—"pulling the 'ool over their eyes," as I heard the economics professor say. This last I sincerely wished had been true, for winter was approaching, and the poor suffer more from cold than from the terrific heat of summer. The garments I distributed were mostly cotton.

During my absences in Flower Town, Balu, my cook—that cheerful poisoner—reigned supreme in my beloved hut. I did not mind the parties he gave there while I was gone, but I did mind his opening the packages that came for me. They contained the clothes in question, and (according to a letter from my sister) some quite decent dolls and toys for poor children; but I never saw these things. I was sure Balu was disposing of as many of them as he dared, to his own advantage. Not only did he protest his innocence, but he took this occasion to announce his engagement to a young lady of eight years (he himself was between twelve and eighteen, depending on his stratagem of the moment), and to remind me that I had promised him a handsome present for his wedding! I could remember no such promise, but I did not deny it, for there was a faint possibility that I had, while learning Bengali, made such a commitment without knowing it; besides, it seemed appropriate that I give him a wedding gift, promise or no promise. I merely let him know that if he ever again in any way confused the contents of the packages with his wedding gift, I would give him a pounding. And I could not help bringing to his attention the fact that the free Santals whom he scorned— Sudra that he was!—neither lie nor steal.

Long-suffering Arjuna babu, who knew yards of English poetry by rote, was now almost my only connection with the outside world. And my relations with him were somewhat strained because I could not take him with me to Flower Town, but kept my life there a secret from him. For he was, after all, a policeman, and the Santals are chary of all officials; but he was also too much the Aryan overlord in spite of his liberalism, and too conscious of being the heir of an ancient, exclusive Brahmanical civilization. The Santals might have accepted him as my friend; at the same time they might have assumed that I shared some of his attitude of the Conqueror toward them, which I did not.

Staying first with Shukdev, then with Buden, I entered into the life of the tribe as if they were my long-lost people. Although the cold winds were beginning to sweep down from the Himalayas, the sky was very blue and clear, and the sun, though high, tanned my white skin brown. Dressed—or rather undressed—like the others, in breechclout and crimson headcloth, barefoot, with beads and amulets thoughtfully provided by Shukdev's mother, I went hunting with my friends. They could bring down a rabbit at forty paces by snaking a blunt arrow along the ground and knocking him on the head with it. The only things I could hit were wild pigs and low-flying bats, and I think I could have got them just as well with a long pole.

There were dances, at the slightest pretext. Every few nights the drums and the flutes would start up. Irresistibly everyone was drawn into the dance—the young and the not so young. Quite little girls attached themselves to the line of women. Boys of ten and fourteen, leaping and fluting like fauns, skittered among the men, daring the mystery of woman. Those who stood beside the great black caldron were soon lying blissfully prone beside it. And was there ever a night or a day when the little flutes and the deep flutes did not converse through the forest?

They were poets, bards, musicians, storytellers. Through Myth they told me of the creation of the world, the nature of things, the reasons for different forms of life, and for different races, sexes, temperaments, and tribal ways. Everything that was had life in it, and a miraculous history. And, not content with the profusion of nature, they boldly envisioned creatures and situations too whimsical even for actuality, though not for self-transcending Truth.

One night there was an especially glorious festival in Flower Town. The occasion was the marriage of Modhu, one of the daughters of Shurja, to a youth from a neighboring tribe. All day the drums and the flutes had been going strong; the great black caldron was flowing; and the dancers had settled into a continuous easy, almost hypnotic motion which they would keep up for several days and nights. Omens and auguries had set the time for the ceremony at about ten o'clock that night. The bridegroom's tribe had arrived in full regalia, wrapped in big shawls of various colors, against the cold. Both men and women wore scarlet hibiscus flowers in their hair or stuck through holes in the lobes of their ears. The women wore the family wealth in the form of silver bracelets, anklets, and necklaces.

Modhu was in strict seclusion in her father's house—that is, her sole companions were some fifteen maidens; no male was permitted to look upon her. This was the first step in the fantastic dramatization of her virginity. At about four o'clock in the afternoon the bridegroom and his cronies attempted to break in and carry away the bride by force, the implication being that such a jewel of virtue, rather than submit to a man, would otherwise escape into the jungle before the ceremony. The bride's relatives, including Shukdev and Buden, thwarted this abduction, during which fists flew and the bridegroom got a bloody nose. Two sets of guards were posted around Shurja's hut: their men, to see that she did not run away, and our men, to see that she was not kidnaped.

The bridegroom had to pass tests in archery, wrestling, stick fighting, broad jumping, and dancing. This was followed by an intimate physical examination and a horoscope. The priest, or medicine man, though a shamanist, was influenced in some ways by Hindu tradition when it came to the ceremony. After interminable auguries had been cast and a great many spirits had been propitiated, he seated the bridegroom, dressed in a white dhoti, before the sacred fire and commanded that the bride be brought in. Seven conch shells moaned three times. The drums stopped so that Modhu's screams could be heard by all. There was a great uproar at Shurja's house. At the last minute Modhu's brothers and cousins were trying to save her by kidnaping her themselves. They fought the good fight—and it was a pretty ugly one, from what I could see by squinting one eye—but they were finally overcome by the superior numbers and determination of the bridegroom and his men.

Once again the bridegroom resumed his seat before the sacred fire. Slowly, triumphantly, his brothers and cousins approached, carrying a huge basket with a lid on it, which contained the bride. Twice en route she succeeded in forcing up the lid, leaning out, looking quite disheveled, and giving a series of operatic screams. They stuffed her in again and clamped the lid down more firmly.

Seven times they carried her around the bridegroom while the priest chanted and shuffled the sacred objects on the ground. Then, raising the lid of the basket, they got hold of the end of her sari and tied it tightly to the end of the bridegroom's dhoti, although she was tugging at it all the while. Modhu gave up. Sulkily she clambered out of the basket and sat down beside her husband, leaning away from him, however, and hiding her face. Once, when Modhu forgot herself and looked at him—it was supposed to be the first time she had ever seen him, although we knew better—we all sighed, or felt like sighing, for she was beautiful and he was handsome and they were both very happy.

After the bridal party had left, taking Modhu off to her new home, I sat with my friends in Shurja's hut, feasting and drinking and telling ribald stories. Shukdev proposed that we ambush the bridal party in the jungle and bring Modhu back; but the priest said it could not be done without antagonizing the spirits, who were enjoying the hashish with which he had lightly drugged them. It could be done in the morning, he said. We all felt that that would be too late to save Modhu.

Drums and flutes and the eternal humming song in three notes made a waterfall of sound in the night. Around the bonfires the long lines of women were swaying and nodding, and within their semicircles the men were leaping fantastically, half-menacingly.

The remaining three daughters of Shurja entered the hut and stood smiling, looking at one another but joking with the young men. The light from the hearth fire and from the guttering oil lamps played over the forms of the three women. With the scarlet flowers in their blue-black hair, eyes like those of forest creatures, round, perfect faces, magnificent bodies—although I might, at one time, have complained of the narrowness of those hips—they were like ebony goddesses. I loved them and I would marry one of them, or perhaps all three of them, and I would live my life in Flower Town, loved and loving, and my children would run naked in the forest and wear flowers in their hair. . . .

Something on the white shawl I was wearing caught my eye. About two feet long, it lay on my shoulder and across my chest, gleaming in that fitful light. It was a golden hair. Slowly I plucked it off and held it up between my thumb and forefinger. A sudden chill came over me.

"Whose hair is this?" I demanded with a harshness I did not intend, for my throat muscles had constricted.

The others stared at it in silence, uncertainly, perhaps a bit sullenly. Their ancient enemies and conquerors, the Aryans, had had golden hair—and nothing is wholly forgotten in India. Then Shurja laughed and clapped me on the knee.

"Nobody has hair like that!" he shouted. "It is a gold thread from a Banaras sari! Ho, ho! Look at those girls of mine—better than a Banaras woman, eh? You are very drunk. So am I!" He rocked with laughter and spilled liquor into everybody's cup.

For them the awkward moment had passed. For me it did not pass. Something had happened to me. My brain whirled with wild speculations, with dread and longing. I wound the golden hair around my finger and sat trying to keep up appearances. It was useless. My mood was affecting the company, or something was. Muttering excuses, I got up and left. Under a cold full moon I cycled back to Bharatpur, stopping every once in a while to stare at the golden hair.

Back in my own hut, I pulled Balu out of bed and demanded an accounting: He had laid out my clothes. Had he seen a golden hair like this? No, Sahib, never! Had he seen a woman with hair like this—anywhere? Never. What of the foreign women who had come to the university before I came? Or were there any new ones? No, none. Anyway, Sahib, it was not a hair but a gold thread. Nobody had hair like that. Would Sahib sleep now? It was two in the morning.

But it was a hair. And it was the most beautiful hair I had ever seen in my life—fine and strong and of the purest gold color! Not flaxen or blonde or copper red, but gold, gold!

I lay down, but I did not sleep that night. Like a scientist re-constructing a prehistoric creature out of a single vertebra, I, myth maker, constructed a visionary creature out of one golden hair. Her beauty surpassed that of all other women, and I wor-shiped her as the goddess of creation. Then it was I knew why Homer, the supreme poet, never attempted to describe Helen, but merely remarked that for such a woman a war was well worth the fighting. With my soul I saw her and I loved her.

The next day I made such exhaustive inquiries about women with golden hair that some people thought me mad. I remem-bered a place Arjuna and I had once found: a crumbled mansion in a desert where a river had been, and the graveyard of an Eng-lish family; but the latest date on the tombstones had been 1892. I questioned Balu closely about the dolls in the packages, for a ludicrous notion struck me at one point, that it might be a doll's hair—but I quickly rejected this. One man told me of a Swede with a long, golden beard who had been at Bharatpur. I knew this was sacrilege, but I checked with Arjuna to make absolutely certain. Of course it was not true. He had had a straw-colored beard, and he had been gone for years. Besides, it was ridiculous to suppose that such a hair had come from any man. It was the golden hair of Helen.

I kept it in a little leather box that I had bought in Venice, and I remembered that the women of that city had once been re-nowned for their beautiful copper-red hair. I took it out many times a day to look at it. At night Helen walked the parapets of Troy.

The cold wind was blowing constantly now, day and night, not violently but enough to rustle the thatched roof, to moan in the tamarind tree that grew against my hut, and to rattle the doors and shutters. There was no letup. Little things began to irritate me, even to send me into sudden rages. For the first time I began to hate the insects. One morning I sacked Balu for shortchanging me on some provisions I had sent him to buy—I had permitted him to cheat me a dozen times before, without deigning to notice. On the afternoon of the same day, I offended Arjuna babu over some trifling matter.

Only five days had passed since my discovery of the golden hair, and I was alone in the world—for I could not go back to Flower Town. My other life was working in me with a vengeance made terrible by my having slighted it for so long. Never again could I enter the Garden.

At five o'clock that afternoon I took the golden hair out of its box for the last time. Winding it around my finger as I had on the first night, I walked out on the desert toward the village of Adityapur, which lies some four miles distant from Bharatpur. The wind was blowing sand and dust and bits of leaves about my ears, and the sun had an odd platinum look. Standing there in the middle of nowhere, in that eery light, with my Indian clothes whipping about me, I unwound the golden hair from my finger, held it up for a moment, then let it go into the wind. . . .

Two years and half a world have come between me and That. Nightly my dreams are still of one whose beauty, though veiled— or because it is veiled—is so poignant that I protest in my sleep. It may be that there is no escape, even in seeking, from that which we most desire.

✦⟨✦⟨✦⟨✦⟨✦⟨✦⟨✦⟨✦⟨ *Jawaharlal and the Three Cadavers*

> "He will forsake everything in the service of man-
> kind, endure every sorrow patiently, not because
> men are suffering and sorrow-laden, but because
> they are beautiful."
>
> —Nasrul Islam, *Mritya Kshudha*

Just before dawn, six black aboriginal women,
walking like barefoot queens along the dusty road, had come
bearing baskets of fresh cow dung on their heads. In the sacred
mango grove at the university they swept off a suitable area; then,
mixing the dung with mud and water, they plastered the ground
with it—and all the while they were singing in unison, their lips
scarcely moving, a song that had only three notes, three that were
really one, like the humming of the earth in summer. Sometimes
they laughed their dark laughter, calling out the ironic secrets
of happiness in a language that no one ever bothered to learn.
In a little while the ground was dry enough for the Hindu girl
students to begin work. Painstakingly, in a thousand-year-old tradition, they traced, with their fingers big elaborate circular designs in white on the paper-like surface of the cow dung. Here the
honored guests would sit.

Prafulla babu, the foreman, elegant in his best white cotton
dhoti, barefoot out of respect for the place and the occasion, was
directing the carpenters as they erected a simple dais. On it they
put rich carpets and a microphone, around which the girls placed
long sticks of incense in fan-like clusters, ready to be lighted.
Bare-legged workmen spread out a great canopy overhead, supported it with bamboo poles, anchored it to branches. It was
woven in stately patterns of yellow, red, and white. Swinging

18

from the tops of mango trees, here and there, were loud-speakers.

Out of the unceasing murmur of conversation, one magic word, a name, occurred again and again: Jawaharlal—which, in those parts, sounds like Johorlal. Affectionately, half-humorously, possessively, "the little people" were calling their prime minister by his first name. Sri Jawaharlal Nehru, Prime Minister of India, Pearl of the Universe, and Chancellor of Bharat University, would arrive at 10:45 A.M., address the assembled faculty, student body, and visitors at 11:00, meet selected persons at a reception in the vice chancellor's house at 11:30, and depart at noon. Sri Jawaharlal was very busy.

Aretino Scott was also busy, laying out his best clothes and—the Plan. Since he was teaching European literature at the university, or was supposed to (and since he was good to look upon, with his auburn hair and his fine dark, intelligent eyes, and could be introduced as "the distinguished American scholar"), he would be at the reception. And there he would lay before the most powerful man in India his Self-Help Plan for the Rehabilitation of Beggars.

Of all the horrors that had confronted Aretino in India, the beggars were the worst. At Jubbulpore, on the third day of his arrival in India, they had laid siege to his second-class railway compartment in which he sat alone. First he had given them his food, then, bit by bit, all the money he had on his person. Thirty, forty, fifty of them appeared out of nowhere. Miauling and mooing, coughing and gibbering, showing sores and stumps, white eyes and black tongues, they swarmed over the carriage, demanding more and yet more of him—demanding everything, everything, even himself!

He bolted the doors, but they bulged in at the windows, scrabbling through the iron bars. He pulled down the shutters, the screens, the glass. They hammered and scratched on the sides of the carriage, howling like animals. Aretino locked himself in the filthy toilet and sat there sweating, reciting Dante, until the train pulled out of fabled Jubbulpore.

Calcutta had been worse. As Aretino walked down Chowringhee Avenue, a creature born of woman but shaped like a starfish, squirmed toward him over the sidewalk; a spider-thing ran at him on its hands and nuzzled his legs, whining human words; a blind leper bloomed at him, all stumps and holes and bulbs; a gang of hideous little outcaste girls cornered him and began to drum on their distended bellies, shrieking without reserve.

Leaping suddenly beyond them, he walked faster and faster, but he could not outdistance them. A soft thing pressed into his side—the head of a scabrous infant held by a woman who was running along beside him. "*Your* baby, Sahib!" she screamed over and over. "*Your* baby!" Other things converged expertly on him. It was a kind of game.

In an agony of the spirit Aretino howled back at them. At least they might leave him his sanity! Fury took the place of pity—he would give them nothing, nothing under such duress! His Scottish stubbornness was aroused, not only against the beggars but also against something in himself—a little heritage from his Venetian mother: it was the ghost of St. Francis of Assisi.

At Bharat University, far in the interior, away from the cities, all was serene. In the atmosphere of the place there still lingered something of the old days when this had been a hermitage. At the end of October, Aretino moved his few belongings—a bedroll, a suitcase, and a box of books—into the Abode of the Foreign Scholars. This square pink block of a building contained four rooms with a common veranda running along in front of them. There were iron bars on the windows to protect the inside from the outside. Each room contained a broad wooden bench to sleep on, a chair, a table, a bookcase, and a foreign scholar. A few trees and a great deal of long, brown grass surrounded the Abode.

Other houses and the university buildings stood at discreet distances.

All was well—until Friday morning at eleven, the time for Aretino's midday meal, which he took at a little table by the window in his room. As he settled down to his rice and curry, he heard a shuffling of bare feet; then, rising from abysmal depths, a blood-curdling groan, with a background of moribund whimpers and whoops.

"*Ba-a-a-a-a-a-bu-u-u-u-u-u-u-u!*"

Standing just outside his window, glaring in at him through the bars, their faces only slightly above the level of his table, were the three most nightmarish creatures he had ever seen in his life: ghoulish old crones, cadavers risen from the grave—"white-eyed phantasms weeping tears of blood."

The first one had shoulder-length hennaed hair, marvelously tousled, and one white eye. The other eye was so crafty that it alone marked her as the brains of the outfit. Every few minutes she wrestled with nearly fatal spasms through which God alone pulled her each time, that she might bear witness as to who were the misers in this world and who were the meritorious.

The second Fury had two teeth and both of them were eye-teeth and both were fangs—since the rest of the mouth had retreated—which rested comfortably on each side of her chin, outside, of course. These fangs were extremely effective when she skinned her lips back, opened her mouth wide, and roared a death-rattle cough. She was cross-eyed and pock-marked, with a crew cut that signified widowhood. She had an air of melancholy.

The third one kept her head swathed in a gray rag. Stepping forward at dramatic moments, she snatched the rag off to show two wildly rolling eyes and a fine leprosy hole in her face where a nose had been. Her few teeth were red and black from chewing betel nut. She had a boyish bob—that is, she too was a widow but she needed a haircut.

Behind the Three Cadavers were the supporting cast: a dozen, fifteen, with painted-on sores and cultivated staggers. And all these actors and actresses were curiously graceful.

Aretino sat frozen in his chair. His hair made a move to escape. Ruthlessly the caterwauling continued. The evil dream spread itself. From the window it moved on to the veranda which Aretino shared with the other foreign scholars. "*Ba-a-a-a-a-a-bu-u-u-u-u-u-u-u!*" it quavered. *Ba-a*, like a lamb on the block, *boo* like the gibbering dead. And *babu* was supposed to mean merely "sir" or "mister"!

Considerably demoralized, Aretino stumbled out on the veranda. There he saw, inside the next room, U Aung, the Burmese scholar, sitting at his desk. Pali scriptures were spread out before him, but he had a mirror in one hand, tweezers in the other, and he was pulling hairs out of his chin. Through the bars on his window he grinned out at Aretino, ignoring the beggars. Doors and shutters of the other two rooms had just been tightly sealed, and Aretino turned to face the beggars alone, when suddenly one of the doors flew open with a crash. The austere Dr. Wilhelm Fraunhofer burst out, wild-eyed and furious.

"Holy God in Heaven!" he screamed. "Get out! Get out!"

Greatly stimulated by these sensitive reactions, the Cadavers and their crew yowled and mewed with incredible vigor. They positively cavorted in their eagerness to celebrate their infirmities. "You are our father and our mother," they gargled; "we are your little children. You are God and we are dirt. Oh, my son, my son! We are your mother and father, you are our dear little baby—"

"Horror!" shrieked the German scholar, who, unfortunately, knew all languages. "I am not your baby; you are not my baby! Go! Go, or I will kill you!"

The Three Cadavers hooted with delight and clawed back their rags to expose leathery breasts hanging down like bats.

Aretino brought out his lunch and gave it to them, plate and all, together with some bananas, a piece of bread, and some coins. They thanked him with dignity, stowed his tribute about their persons, and, in a business-like way, began to hammer on Dr. Fraunhofer's door—for he had again retreated within his room.

Soon a coin slid out to them from under the closed door. They examined it and recommenced their banging and booing. Another coin came, then another. There was a brief consultation, a flutter of grisly eyelashes in Aretino's direction, and they turned to attack the Turk.

Ali Bey's doors and shutters remained tightly sealed all through the siege—and it was a lengthy one, for beggars are rich in time. Aretino watched them finally hobbling away with their booty, chatting animatedly.

Cautiously Dr. Fraunhofer opened his door. "It is characteristic of these people!" shouted the authority on the Sanskrit aorist. "The authorities of the university should not permit such things. My schedule of research has been inexcusably interrupted. I have protested. Nothing is done. In Germany the authorities would take action—*immediately*!"

The little Turk, who really knew no languages but Turkish, emerged from his room, his bush of black whiskers quivering, his great black soulful eyes afloat in their own whites.

"Dees *créatures*," he hissed in French and English, which he used interchangeably, "dey are wot you name like *revenants— sortis du tombeau*. All Fridays dey *arrivent*. *Que faire—moi?* My *tempérament*"—he laid his hand with a gentle crushed motion on his heart—"is *tendre*. I am not *capable* to *supporter* deir cries, deir frapping on my *porte*. I *cache* myselves in de latrine, I seat, I attend, my *doigts* in my *oreilles*."

U Aung appeared in his doorway, grinning, still holding the mirror and the tweezers.

"May I invite you to take tea with me, gentlemen?" he asked.

It was a mystery that Aretino never was able to solve definitely, that the beggars came only on Fridays. Surely no one had given them permission to come at all, and probably no one had been so foolish as to forbid them to come—one would have lost face;

for the beggars, having nothing to lose, were sovereign rebels, as free as the little dawn wind. It seemed likely that they had a regular weekly schedule which took them from village to village, and on Fridays they covered the university area—coming to the Abode of the Foreign Scholars in time for lunch.

But it was difficult to explain their strange punctuality—in India, of all places. The most disturbing thought was that perhaps these exaggerated creatures had, after all, a sense of moderation in that they swooped down only at certain stated intervals. The implication was that one should be grateful for their restraint and that this gratitude ought naturally to take tangible form. To such scruples one could only respond with a lively sense of *dharma*, or duty; and if one failed, it was fitting that one be haunted into conformity.

To Aretino Scott it was moral blackmail. To Dr. Fraunhofer it was one more proof of the evil to which the world had condemned itself by defeating Germany. Ali Bey was confirmed in his view of the world as tragic, insecure, and unclean. And U Aung, with his Buddhist belief that all suffering springs from desire—or fear—of that which is illusory, regarded it all with cheerful detachment.

And it was always a crisis. What attitude, what policy ought one to have? For the beggars would seldom yield short of victory. It was necessary to decide in advance of the hysteria which they knew so well how to produce. The difficulty was in being consistent. If Aretino was to give, he ought to keep on giving; soon, like St. Francis, he would have nothing left and he would join the beggars, adding one more to their number. And perhaps it would be easier to possess nothing, easier to bedevil others!

After several months of Fridays had come and gone, a pattern of conduct began to take shape: The beggars would come at meal-time. Aretino would go out on the veranda and face them, a tight knot of panic in his solar plexus; then he would give them all the food he had on his table or in his room, and several annas apiece.

In all the welter of loathing and pity and abortive ideas, he had the obscure conviction that this was, after all, the least incorrect thing he could do until he had settled on a policy.

From Aretino they would go to U Aung, who, plucking hairs out of his illusory chin, would cheerfully ignore the illusory throng. They wasted little time on him. With great verve they summoned the German to his doom. After a few minutes of their caterwauling, death-rattling, and banging on his shutters, Dr. Fraunhofer in torment would come bursting out of his sealed room, curse and threaten, and retreat once more, only to slide the extortion money out under the door.

Although they never had any success at the opposite end of the Abode of Foreign Scholars, the beggars always gave special attention to the tightly closed room in which Ali Bey huddled in frozen silence, his fingers in his ears. After "the treatment" was over and the beggars had passed like an evil gray wave, Ali Bey the Lacerated would stumble out, his face ghastly, to establish contact again with human beings—that is, with Aretino the Faint, Wilhelm the Furious, and U Aung the Detached.

Early one Friday morning, before the beggars came, Aretino stood on the veranda and addressed the Foreign Scholars: "Gentlemen," he said, "this is Friday. We are about to receive a horrible visit. Do you not think we should meet this situation with a little common sense?"

Ali Bey's eyes flashed with a noble passion. Moved beyond words, he stretched himself to his full height of five feet four, and impetuously gave Aretino a Turkish military salute.

U Aung giggled happily and prepared to make tea.

"I assume that you have a new contribution to make," said Dr. Wilhelm Fraunhofer, "otherwise you would not have walked out upon the veranda to address me, as well as these other two men, at this particular moment, thereby implying a conviction on your part that there exists a consideration which outweighs in importance any possible research which we may be engaged in doing, and the sober knowledge that an error in your judgment may have permanent, pronounced results upon the fruition of our work?"

Aretino said: "I propose an orderly plan for dealing with the beggars. It will render justice to them and to us, and it will save you from being disturbed so much. The disturbance it causes me is my concern. All I ask is that you make me your exclusive agent. Give me the money you would give to them, and do not laugh or interfere in any way. Ask no questions. Stay in your rooms. I shall assume complete responsibility for action—although you are all morally implicated."

They stared at him in silence. Then, solemnly, Dr. Fraunhofer counted out eight annas into Aretino's hand; Ali Bey gave him four annas; and U Aung, who would give the beggars nothing, gave two annas for sociability and metaphysical entertainment.

There were about a dozen beggars in the first wave. Foremost among them, as always, were the most hideous—the Three Cadavers. Aretino stood on the veranda and faced them with his palms together, fingers pointing up as in prayer, in the polite greeting of *namaskar*. Poised for the onslaught, they were momentarily checked by the sahib's unprecedented behavior. Slowly, unevenly they returned his *namaskar*, and during this pause Aretino addressed them in careful Bengali phrases which he had worked out during the preceding weeks.

"All those in this house have given me money to give to you," he said. "I alone speak to you in the name of all."

The Three Cadavers looked at one another; the False Leper looked at the False Fakir; Old Harelip looked at the woman with the guilty baby; the guilty baby looked fixedly at the sun; and the sun looked down on all of them and was very big and very hot. The sahib had addressed them as *apni*—the polite pronoun which one uses only with equals or with superiors. It was unheard of, yet the sahib was not laughing. How embarrassing! And there was something in his statement which, by implication, threatened their freedom of action. Enough of this nonsense!

"*Ba-a-a-a-a-a-bu-u-u-u-u-u-u-u!*" they keened, once more beginning to limp and stagger and exhibit. "Give us the money! God will reward you. Give us food, give us clothing—"

"Give *me* something," Aretino said, "then I will give you something in exchange. That will be right."

"O babu! Do not be cruel! What have *we* to give? Nothing— nothing!"

"You can work. Do a little work, and I will pay you."

"Babu! *Babu-u-u-u-u!*" the practiced gibbering began again. "We are dying. We cannot work. Look at us."

It was true, they were in rather poor condition, but . . .

"You have walked five miles this morning," Aretino said, "in order to beg. If you can walk, you can work."

"No, no, babu! What work can *we* do?"

Pitilessly he pointed at the dry grass in front of the Abode of the Foreign Scholars.

"Pull grass," he said. "I desire grass. Pull grass for me, and I will pay you."

It was beginning to be apparent that the sahib had cracked under the strain of his own obstinacy. Already several of the beggars were edging away. Aretino marched down the steps, across the yard, squatted down, and began to pull grass, laying it in a pile.

"Do this," he said, "only for a little while."

The orange-robed false priest smiled pityingly. "My son," he said, "I am a Brahman. I cannot do such work."

"Permit me to do it for you," said Aretino.

The priest and most of the others straggled away.

"Stay," Aretino called after them. "Please stay. Work for only fifteen minutes. Ten minutes."

The Three Cadavers and a few others remained, with expressions of extreme distrust.

"What will you give us?" It was the henna-haired hag with the crafty eye.

"An anna a minute, for ten minutes."

"Ten rupees for ten minutes," the hag countered. If the young sahib was mad enough to give ten annas for such a trifle, he was mad enough to give ten rupees. Besides, there was a little matter of professional pride, for which ten rupees would scarcely compensate.

"No," Aretino said with an injured air as he walked back to the veranda. "You don't want to work. No work, no money. *Namaskar.*"

"Wait, Sahib," the hag with fangs said. "You mean—like this?" With great dignity she squatted down and yanked at the grass. Reluctantly the other two hags creaked down beside her. They looked at one another and began to titter like schoolgirls: they had stepped out of character—into this world, as it were. A spook, after all, was somebody—and now they had allowed themselves to be inveigled into the most prosaic kind of work!

"Like that," Aretino said, looking ostentatiously at his watch.

The False Leper joined them, and then Old Harelip. The young woman with the baby looked meaningfully at the handsome sahib with the ivory skin and the auburn hair; he ignored her, so she too began to pull grass, groaning, however.

Aretino timed each of them, and saw that they worked steadily. At the end of their ten minutes he gave each of them ten annas.

"Ten rupees, Sahib!" the hennaed hag chanted, but without conviction.

"Come again on Friday," he said. "I shall expect you."

When Friday came again, there were forty beggars, not a dozen. Aretino's fame had spread—the mad sahib gave a day's wages for ten minutes' work and a few handfuls of grass, for which he must have an inexplicable passion! He was forced to cut wages and shorten hours: five annas for five minutes. In his eagerness to organize, he had nearly been swallowed by his own machine.

Nevertheless they came. The piles of dry grass grew bigger and bigger in front of the Abode of the Foreign Scholars. Coldly, inflexibly he stood on the veranda and exacted from them their

five minutes of work. Then he paid them with scrupulous exacti-
tude, dropping the coins into their claws from as great a height
as practicable, squinting his eyes in order to blur the hideous
vision.

One morning when Aretino was making his weekly collection
from the scholars, Fraunhofer glanced keenly at his face and
barked out in that harsh accent:

"This was a good idea, Scott—for us, here, now. You love these
beggars, eh?"

"*Love?*" Aretino cried. "What do you want for your money?"

"Why don't you admit that you hate and despise them, that
they are vermin and should be destroyed?"

For a moment Aretino had a vision of a mass grave. It was
distinctly pleasing.

"Not convenient, eh?" Fraunhofer pursued.

"Not—imaginative."

"*Ach!* You want to perform a metamorphosis! To make good
bourgeois out of them, *ja?* You want to destroy their identity, as
I do—to destroy them as beggars and as problems whose only
mission is to destroy *us*. We differ only in method. For you,
reform. For me, extermination. But let there be no pious pretense
between us, eh?"

Aretino considered passionately while Dr. Fraunhofer, with an
ironic smile, counted out eight annas for him.

One night, out of a dream of beggars, he was awakened by a
hellish uproar of jackals. The moonlight was beating down on
his sweat-bathed face, through the mosquito curtain, with an
intense white-cold urgency. Out there, beyond the dry grass, he
glimpsed a fantastic ballet of small dog-like animals, leaping and
swirling over one another, all nerves, tropisms, hysteria. A yelling,
shrieking, unrestrained, competitive madness! And it was all
trying to take place within himself.

"Beasts!" he gasped. "God-damned beasts! Put 'em in a pen and
feed 'em—out of earshot!" It was partly the moon, the leprous

moon. Throw a gray rag over it, jerk it back every few minutes —that'll reduce the will to breed!

And a wall. Provide for them but build a wall, an unclimbable soundproof wall, with them on the other side, fat, playful, neutralized horrors. And then life can be lived. . . . In this land the ears have walls, and the mind, the mind—Lord, everything does, and walls breed walls. But this would be the wall to end all walls —the Great Wall of India.

Then, obedient to his will, out of the yowling tangle of moonlight, there unfolded before him a Vision of Order. Serene and clear and antiseptic, of classical simplicity, it pictured in outline a series of centers throughout India, where all the beggars would be brought together. There, under supervision, they would construct their own shelters, spin and weave their own cloth according to the method advocated by Mahatma Gandhi, and produce their own food. And they would govern themselves as free men and women, proud and self-sufficient. Until then—seal them off!

From that night on, he devoted many hours to thought and research, culminating in the Self-Help Plan for the Rehabilitation of Beggars. Nothing was left out, from the methods of compelling and attracting the beggars to the centers, and keeping them there, to their ultimate conversion to normality and absorption into society. And even then the centers would always remain as prosperous model villages ready to receive all kinds of refugees into their flexible economies.

"The Self-Help Plan for the Rehabilitation of Beggars will rid India of this evil and this disgrace once for all," Aretino said firmly, summing up his eloquent appeal. Sri Abanindranath Basu, the Calcutta bicycle magnate and philanthropist, waggled his head, his breasts, his stomach, his legs, and slithered his hands and feet, to convey the feeling that there was no stiffness in his attitude. He continued to keep his head loose on his neck and to wiggle his plump thighs, swathed in rather sheer white cotton cloth. The unselfconscious sensuality of his rhythms was discomfiting.

Carefully, even apologetically, he explained to Aretino that the idealistic Plan would founder upon a still higher idealism—or at least an older one: The devout Hindu needed beggars to fulfill his *dharma*. In giving to them he was passing a test in this particular life. The rewards would be reaped in subsequent lives, in higher births, probably. So the beggar served a purpose in life, and his being was justified. The exchange between beggar and donor was exactly equivalent; both were benefactors, both in need. . . . Not that he, Mr. Basu, took much stock in such shenanigans, but nearly everybody else did.

Other businessmen were courteous; they led Aretino into abstruse discussions, quoted yards of poetry, and ended by making commitments as obliging and indeterminate as the roads of India. The climate, the strangeness, the ambiguities of the land spun webs of Maya around him and his shining Plan. He could only brood over it in solitude and perfect it on paper for the day when somebody with power, somewhere, would put it into effect.

Meanwhile he was the steady employer of beggars, a dealer in dry grass. At first he had given it to the passing aboriginal women, thinking they might use it to start their fires with. But after several such transactions he caught their amused glances at one another, and he realized that they were carrying it off out of charity. No one wanted the grass. Bitterly, in secret, he paid a farmer to haul it away in a bullock cart.

Now, after several months of frustration, during which he had neglected his other work and had been joined only by a colony of bacilli in his small intestine, there was a sign of hope: The prime minister was coming to the university, and the foreign scholars were to meet him. The logic of events was evident. Aretino was aware that stage fright might make him bungle and that boldness might make him seem officious; it could not be helped: this was his unique opportunity to present the Self-Help

Plan. For Jawaharlal was not only the highest authority in India
—after the People, of course—he was also a sensitive human being
with, thank God, a secular approach to life.

On the morning of the Day, Aretino was pacing up and down,
a look of triumph on his haggard face. He had been up nearly all
night—aided by his dysentery—formulating a few sentences cal-
culated to arrest Jawaharlal's attention, and perfecting a brief
résumé of the Plan. Once introduced, he would have to work
fast.

Aretino was laying out the white shirt he would wear to meet
Jawaharlal—when the Voice struck:

"*Babu—bikar, bikar, bikar!*"

It was only the chant of Old Harelip, deformed and musical, a
coo, a stammer—so patient. And all it meant was, "Sir, a beggar,
a beggar, a beggar!" Literally that was all it meant, a simple surface thing. But a hidden listener in Aretino, freakishly sensitized
by events and now caught unawares, heard "*babu*" which made
him an Indian or an anybody, not a white sahib, and "*baba*" which
made him a father and protector; and "baby"—himself a world
child, fragmentary and defective, a beggar boy. Thrice he was.
So went that dark, instant exegesis. And the graybeard father,
hoary and indistinct with time and fate, seemed to be telling him,
out of the compassionate wisdom of the Buddha: "Be calm, be
calm, be calm!"

On that sound the will of Aretino Scott pivoted, suddenly and
inexplicably, in a moment of time, and broke. He sat on the floor.
The Great Wall of India fell in ruins about him. When, after
some time, he had composed himself sufficiently, he arose and
went out on the veranda, still clutching the shirt, which was no
longer quite immaculate. Old Harelip, with his staff and his rag
turban and his skinny brown shanks, was squatting out in the
yard, meditatively tugging at a wisp of grass, but it slipped

through his fingers. He turned his filmy eyes on Aretino with a smile of ironic resignation.

"You have worked well," Aretino said softly, and he gave him the white shirt.

The Three Cadavers were over in the grass, working away. They had come quietly, without even announcing their arrival. Gravely they stood up and greeted Aretino with the *namaskar;* then they resumed their work, chatting away and occasionally chuckling.

Aretino was drawn irresistibly toward them. He squatted down near them and began to pull grass.

"The hot months come," he said. "Then what will you do?"

"It will rain and we shall work for you," said the crone with the white eye. "And what will you do, babu?"

"I do not know," said Aretino.

"There will be new grass, green grass. Do you also like green grass?"

"Very much," he quavered.

"Do not sweat your brains, babu," Old White Eye said soothingly. "There is grass enough for all."

When Nandulal brought his meal, Aretino carried it over to the shade of a tree near the Abode of the Foreign Scholars and shared it with the Three Cadavers—Old Harelip had gone on his way.

"Where are the other people who come on Fridays?" Aretino asked when they had finished eating.

"They have all gone to see Jawaharlal, the father of our country," said White Eye.

"We, however, desired to come here," said Fangs, smiling down at her hands. Aretino looked up. The sun was directly overhead. Automatically, propelled by the mere obsessive pattern of the past months, he acted—or rather, was acted upon—carried along like a dead horseman into battle.

With the Self-Help Plan for the Rehabilitation of Beggars under his arm, he reached the road leading to the vice chancellor's residence. A multitude lined both sides of the road. Their voices arose in the distance, then rolled nearer, like flights of birds, exalted into the air like invisible birds.

The crowd sealed him off solidly from the road. And there, all in a group, were his beggars. Very courteously they made room for him, closing after. He took Old Harelip's place in the front rank, just in time. A cloud of dust, like voices visible, billowed up behind an open car as it approached.

"Jawaharlal! Jawaharlal!" they murmured, and "*Jai Hind!*" Long live India!

The great man rode past. For an instant the beautiful dark, intelligent eyes rested on Aretino Scott and the beggars, and then a cloud of dust was where the prime minister had been.

Vacant and unseeing, Aretino returned to the Abode of the Foreign Scholars. For a moment he stood on the veranda, and then he smiled crookedly. On his doorstep was a fine big pile of grass. Really, there was so much!

Of course, they had carried off his dishes. Next time he promised himself, they would have to eat off plantain leaves like ordinary people.

Flight of White Crows

"Thou art born with faces turned in all directions."
—Upanishads

"Which of the ladies shall be first?" The Nepalese clerk in the Rampoche police station was late: but once there, he smiled about him with charming manners. The foreign women in saris made a move toward him simultaneously, each from a different part of the room, then they stopped and looked at Dorsey. "You go first," the Englishwoman said to her. It was the first time one of them had spoken to another since their separate arrivals. "I came last," Dorsey said.

The German woman tore a chair out of a corner and shoved it in front of the clerk's desk. "Sit here! You are in no condition!" Then she retreated, folded her massive arms, and stood motionless. Dorsey sat down slowly.

"Name, please?"

"Dorsey Willet Mukherji."

"Nationality?"

"American."

"Occupation?"

"Housewife."

"Husband's name, nationality, occupation?"

"Nimal Chandra Mukherji, Indian national, employed by UNESCO, presently in Paris . . ."

"We greatly regret this inconvenience to you, Mrs. Mukherji," the clerk said, "but all foreigners must register here. What a pity the word 'foreigner' exists! Dreadful regulations! But, truly, we are not an insensitive people."

"I know you are not." She laughed, and held out her hand to him. He helped her up. As she walked out she smiled her thanks at the silent women. They nodded back encouragingly—all except the one with freckles, who might have been American.

At the door a voice said over her shoulder, "My dear." Dorsey turned and looked into a pair of bright brown eyes—they were perhaps a little too bright. "I beg your pardon for speaking to you, but I wish to inquire if you need help, if you have a doctor, if you are all alone. . . ." She was a thick-set woman of about fifty, perhaps Slavic, and although she inquired, she did not wait for an answer, but continued to speak. "I am Olga Basu, but everyone calls me only by my first name. . . ."

The sky was dropping rain steadily and gently from a few feet overhead, as Dorsey climbed on up the mountain. Evidently one did not walk in this Himalayan town. One climbed: either up or down. That explained the total absence of bicycles. At one corner several Tibetans, looking like American Indians with their big felt hats and braided hair, sheltered themselves from the rain in their two-man rickshaws—covered, ornate relics of Imperial India; but Dorsey refused to ride in a man-drawn vehicle even now, although she could not forget the discussion she had had with Nimal in Calcutta, about taking a rickshaw. The rickshaw puller had turned away in disgust, with the comment: "If all were philosophers like you, we wallahs would starve to death!"

How many additional pounds of rainwater had soaked into the long yards of her sari she could only guess; and yet she must wear a sari. Like a wedding ring, it was a visible sign that she affirmed India—even though India did not affirm her. Things were so difficult! Even the big black umbrella she carried—a concession to the Third Person she contained—was a mark of social prestige. Village Brahmans carried them unfurled over their sacred locks on the balmiest summer nights! A pang of guilt struck her at the thought of those Brahmans and the untouchables and everyone in between, being parboiled alive down there on the plains. If only the monsoon rains would come to them now!

Minna

The breathless German woman, bareheaded in the rain, came laboring up the mountainside to Dorsey's cottage. Instead of knocking at the door, she lurked at the window, Indian fashion —that is, "informally"—until Dorsey came and opened the window.

"I am Minna Chakravarty. I cannot come in just now—the rain is nothing—but I shall come this evening, if you will permit. I heard you invite Olga Basu to tea this afternoon, and I wanted to speak to you about her. She has had a nervous breakdown—she is still having one—and she is very emotional. Do not let her upset you, and do not take seriously the things she will tell you."

"Really, I—"

"You are alone here?"

"I have a maid."

"Send her to me when you need anything. Have you a doctor?"

"Not yet, I—"

"It isn't necessary. I never had a doctor with any of mine, and I've had seven. I will help you. However, Dr. Chowdhury is in Rampoche, and I will establish contact between you, in case you want him. It will be soon, won't it?"

"Very soon," Dorsey said.

"Ah," said Minna Chakravarty, "we must be careful. And remember what I told you about poor Olga Basu. Change the subject whenever she starts to get excited—and you should not ask her back. I will return tonight, and we can make plans."

"Yes, but come in and dry off," Dorsey said. "You look so wet!"

"It is nothing," Minna said with a little twist of her oiled blonde head. Her mannerisms, as well as the intonations of her English, were neither English nor German, but carefully, studiously Indian. "Then, I am coming," she said, and instead of coming, she went.

It might be nice, Dorsey thought, to be mothered by this generous woman, to entrust everything to her—even though she was a bit domineering. But there was something hidden within all that heartiness: she had little squinty blue eyes that darted away from you and kept their own counsel.

Olga

" I am so glad you have come to Rampoche," Olga said, putting too much sugar in her tea. "You are a person I can talk to—you have understanding. I also am an intellectual. I have lived a very full life, in every sense of the word, and I wish to share my experience with you, to help you—for I can see that you need help, whereas my life is dedicated to service. You are new in India, are you not? One year! Yes, you are very new. I have been here for thirty years this time; before—thousands of years! But you do not believe in reincarnation? Never mind, you will." She laughed a strong, musical laugh and leaned forward in her chair. "Do you know how I recognized you? It was your laugh, there in the police station. I could not resist speaking to you. You have courage, like me. Perhaps I can show you the way to Self-Realization. My guru taught me everything. He was my husband. You see, I am a widow." Letting the border of her white sari fall back from her head, she revealed her hair cropped short according to the custom of Hindu widows. Olga turned her weathered profile to Dorsey and rested her gaze on the unmelting snows of Kinchinjunga, the mountain that dominates that part of the world.

"He was a man. God's mercy on those who did not know his love. God's mercy on those who did." Olga paused, looked searchingly at Dorsey, and laughed a throaty, secret laugh: "And what about your little man, my dear?"

"Please excuse me," Dorsey said. "I'm feeling a bit tired."

"Oh, yes! You must lie down," Olga said, jumping up abruptly and making for the door. Then, coming part way back, she said in a confidential tone: "There is a woman in Rampoche who may try to turn you against me by misrepresenting the facts, since you are a newcomer. She used to be my friend, but she did something very bad. Fearing that I would expose her, she began to defame my character. I am incapable of hatred. I am very sorry for her, but she would not let me help her. She remains sealed up with her own guilt, confiding in no one. Perhaps you can help her, and—I will tell you a little of her case history, since it is widely known anyway, and then you will not be at the mercy of unreliable informants. The truth will give you power to help her, and I shall be eternally grateful to you."

"Perhaps next time?" Dorsey said. "I really am very tired."

"Oh! Yes, of course! Then I will just say: Be kind to Minna Chakravarty. Allow her to help you. It is her life. It is all the life she has—helping people. For many years her husband has prac-ticed brahmachari—complete chastity—and Minna is extremely—well! After the sixth child, he stopped, but Minna wanted to go on, you know. She acted in a scandalous way before men, right in public. Her husband kept her in seclusion, in remote parts of India. Then one day she had a child, a very dark one, darker than her husband, darker than his friends—as dark as the aborigines who lived nearby. Her husband was very angry and he beat her. That night the newborn baby succeeded in jumping out of her arms—out of a second-story window—do you follow me? Minna had a nervous breakdown. Since then she has been very active in women's organizations—social welfare of all kinds, disseminating birth-control information. . . . But, my dear, you need a rest. I shall return often to see if you need something."

The rain had stopped, and a heavy pearly fog filled the world. It had mounted up from below, exactly to the steps of Dorsey's cottage, where it lay like a gray surf. From her islanded house she could see Kinchinjunga floating on the same ocean, over a

quietly depopulated earth. Olga's stout, too energetic figure, en-
folded in the flowing lines of her sari, waded out and down
toward the engulfed town, like some amphibious creature into
abysses containing abysses.

Minna

"Dr. Chowdhury will call on you tomorrow morning at ten
o'clock," Minna said. "He is a very good man, a relative of my
husband's, one of the best physicians in India. And, for your information, I myself have delivered successfully scores of babies
in the past ten years. I have had no complaints."

Hang motives and the past, Dorsey thought. This was a warmhearted person, unselfish, efficient, learned. Her activities covered
everything possible: the arts, science, scholarship, national and
international politics, reform. She was a one-woman bridge between East and West; it wouldn't be a bad idea to pattern one's
own life after hers. If one could not really see her eyes, did it
matter so much?

"Minna," Dorsey said, squeezing her hand, "I am very grateful.
You're a wonderful person. If I can ever help you—"

Roughly, Minna jerked her hand away. Her face was splotched
with red; her upper lip was beaded with sweat. "You don't know
what you are saying! I am not wonderful. I am—very bad."
Again she began to talk, but this time she was irrational. She said
nothing about her private life, but over the wrongs of India, and
especially the atrocities she had seen during the Hindu-Moslem
rioting, and the great famine of 1943—all, she said, engineered by
the British—she became hysterical. The injustices of the world
flooded in upon her—the world's grief became her grief, and she
wept. Then all at once it was finished.

"Forgive me," she said quietly, wiping her eyes. "You will see
many bizarre things in India, and I am one of them. You too will
become one, if you do not run back to America while you still
have time."

"Back to America? Nimal wants me to. He's going from Paris to New York soon. We met in New York, you know, and that's where he thinks we should live. Things would be much easier there, away from India's heat and the insects and the snakes and the squalor and disease and the prejudice—and the loneliness."

"*Ach! Die Einsamkeit!* Go back, woman!"

"I'm not ready to go back, Minna. Not yet. I don't really know India—I haven't got into its life."

"You never will," Minna said. "I know. India will take all the gifts of your love, and she will give you nothing. Oh, yes!" she laughed bitterly. "You will get the giving—you understand, that is what the saints tell us: giving is the great thing. And you will give and give, and you will go mad, and you will die, and it will be as if you had never existed. India will go on like an incurable disease, but you will die of it, and I, and Olga Basu, and Sylvia Chowdhury, and that other little American thing in the police station—Joy Something-or-Other—we shall never be anything but white crows, embarrassed to see one another, shunned by the rest of the flock."

"White crows!" Dorsey could not help laughing at the phrase. "But why embarrassed to see one another?"

Feeling her somber wit appreciated, Minna relaxed and even smiled a little. "I don't know," she said. "Well, yes, I do. In fact, I have made a thorough analysis of it, so I am no longer interested."

"Tell me!"

"No. . . . We resent other Western women here. We fear that they will expose our contradictions by behaving normally. However, it does not last long. If you have no serious defects, India will create them."

"I think I have a White Goddess complex already," Dorsey said. "We ought to organize a union, assign spheres of influence to avoid cramping one another's style."

"You do not take me seriously."

"Sure, I do."

"What did Olga tell you?"

At the other's sudden intensity Dorsey became cautious. "She loved her husband very much. He must have been an extraordinary man."

"He was twice her age, a dried-up little scholar, and—Olga remains an old maid, unhappily. She should have had seven children. Instead, she is a Soviet spy. Didn't she say anything about me?"

"Nothing I can recall offhand," Dorsey lied.

"Very well," Minna said, rising to go. "Then please forget everything I have said."

"I wonder what her eyes would have to say?" Dorsey thought.

Monica

Dorsey was standing on the terrace, looking out over the flower beds, over the roofs of Rampoche, over the chasms and the lunar snow peaks, out to Kinchinjunga: very clear and pure and bright in the morning air; so unattainable that it liberates man to baseness, she thought; so far away, so perfect that there is nothing to connect it with human beings. The hill people worshiped it as God, but it would have to become Man before it could do any good—or any evil. How strange it was that she felt walled in by all that Himalayan magnificence! Over the years the subtle modulations of the plains would be more bearable. The plains did not disfurnish the imagination, nor did the exotic multitude there ever give her the feeling of being treed with all sorts of special creatures. . . . There beyond lay Tibet and Sikkim, the clouded leopard, the musk deer and the moose deer. Below her on the paths wandered Tibetan women with fantastic headdresses, Lepcha women with great baskets on their backs, Nepalese with gold ornaments in their noses. . . .

A dark woman in Western dress looked up at her, and smiled. "Good morning," she said in a cockney-like accent. "I'm your neighbor, Mrs. Pereira—Monica Pereira. Enjoying the view? It's much better in October. You can see Kinchinjunga by moon-light—if you like that sort of thing. It gives me the creeps." She came up the path into the garden and began to admire the roses. "I say"—she looked sidelong at Dorsey—"it must have been beastly hot on the plains to bring you here—in your condition."

"Oh, it was!" Dorsey said. "It hit all at once. I got sick and I was afraid something would happen, so I took a plane to Dwarka and a car from there. Everyone was very careful with me."

"When I see a lot of Europeans arriving at the same time, I know it's beastly hot on the plains."

"Do you live here?" Dorsey inquired.

"Oh, yes." Monica Pereira gestured down the mountain. "My people built this place—out of nothing, they did. See those stone buildings? British!"

For a moment Dorsey had a vision of ruined dynasties—Mohenjodaro and Buddhist and Mogul, Rajput and British—and she felt a curious sympathy for them all. "Once at Chartres," she murmured, "in the cathedral, I had what the Indians might call a darshana—a religious experience, only secular. I said: '*My people did this!*' I felt an immense pride, and the funny thing was, I'm not French at all."

Monica's sharp black eyes looked sideways at Dorsey. "You're American, aren't you? I'm English. I had a Spanish grandfather, though. Next year I'm going home to England—to get away from the Indians."

"I married one," Dorsey said quietly, unwilling to take sides in Monica's private battle.

Monica glanced at her, then quickly looked away. "I never would," she murmured. "The baby might be white, though."

Sylvia

"Yes, I know Monica," Sylvia Chowdhury said. "Why do you ask?" She was a stately, elegant woman in her thirties, with ash-blonde hair and serene gray eyes. Followed by her Nepalese bearer, she had come bringing to Dorsey a beautiful basket of fruit—litchis, mangoes, oranges, peaches, papayas, and Kashmir apples.

"I wondered," Dorsey said. "I have yet to meet a Eurasian—an Anglo-Indian—who doesn't deny the Indian part of his ancestry. It's so stupid. My baby needn't be proud, but I don't want him to be ashamed. Not on this account. Why should the races have to fight in his veins?"

"Things rebel and live. You yourself are in no ordinary position."

"I know," Dorsey said. "My position is still odder here in Rampoche. I feel guilty for having left all those people on the plains to die in the heat. They were suffering just as much as I was. More, because of the summer plagues. I deserted—ran out on them: people I know, people I'm fond of. . . ."

"Survival is nearly always immoral. That's why the British built Rampoche."

Dorsey smiled. "India must have aged the British."

Sylvia Chowdhury gazed at Dorsey out of those cool gray eyes, and there was something in them of the smiling Buddha. "I hope you will stay in India," she said.

"I don't know. The Western women I've met here—how do they manage?"

"It's all on credit. Again, a little matter of survival."

"What will I be in twenty years? I feel I can ask you that. Somehow, I can't ask the others about their lives—not yet, anyway."

Sylvia glanced at her watch and got up to go. "I forgot to tell you," she said pleasantly, "that I'm receiving contributions for an orphanage near Tashiling. They're Anglo-Nepalese waifs they found living like wild animals in the forest. You see, the tea planters hereabout were mostly British, and some are still here— no longer quite so fertile, thank God, but there are still orphans.

And they're such beautiful children! Come and see them. My husband and I have adopted three. We plan to have no children of our own."

Dorsey wrote out a check.

Olga

"You are so big and lovely," Olga said. "Had you thought that you might give birth to a monster?"

"My husband would be exasperated!"

"Do not be dismayed, my dear, no matter what happens. Everything progresses by opposites, as you will learn when you study philosophy. Even a monster might surprise you. Through suffering and glandular maldistribution, monsters often have deep insights into the nature of reality; so we have cultural progress. This is something my sister Katya never understood; instead of fleeing to India with me, at the time of the Revolution, she chose the normality of America. This caused problems which I have been unable to solve for her."

"Your sister lives in America?"

"In Washington, the heart and soul of America. However, she is now traveling somewhere in India with her husband, Professor Karl Fraunhofer, who also became an American. His German brother is at Bharat University in Bengal, doing research on the Sanskrit aorist. Katya is now Katy Fraunhofer, a trusted agent of America. Poor Katya!"

"Why 'poor Katya'?"

"Alas, she is not intelligent enough to succeed as an American agent—and also a Soviet agent. Her mind is beginning to deteriorate."

"Oh, but are you sure she is anybody's agent?"

"Unfortunately, yes. She asked me to help her, but I could not see my way clear, at my age, to become a spy—especially for the communists. Do you remember the young American girl in the police station? She is Joy Davis and she has married into the

Vora family of Calcutta, with whom I am acquainted through my husband. Katya is convinced that the girl is an American agent sent to spy on her. She wanted me to cultivate Joy's friendship and then betray her confidence. I refused. But also I cannot betray Katya to Joy Davis and the American authorities. You may, if you wish."

"What a mess! I don't want to betray anybody. I'm sure the Secret Service knows all about it."

Olga smiled grimly. "The Secret Service would be appalled if it were ever confronted with the essence of things," she said. "However, the pitiable secrets of nations often corrupt people's motives. It might be well for you to be cautious if you meet Joy Davis, since it is apparently her duty to spy on the activities of Americans in India. She should be satisfied if you are not a communist—and perhaps you are one? No? In either case, I advise you to avoid her altogether. As for poor Katya—Katy Fraunhofer!—*nothing* can satisfy her except death. Avoid her absolutely! But should she come to Rampoche, do not be disturbed. I shall protect you from her."

"And Professor Fraunhofer? A Nazi?"

"A harmless reactionary. He thinks he is serving America, but he is serving Katya."

"Your sister must be rich by now, working for both sides?"

"On the contrary, there are persons on both sides to whom she must pay blackmail. You see, she has been indiscreet."

"I suppose she had to be," Dorsey said, "in order to succeed without intelligence."

"America," said Olga, "must be a very strange place indeed."

Minna

Ach! You are discreet," Minna said, "and virtuous too, probably. How is it possible to be both? However, I asked Dr. Chowdhury to send his wife, Sylvia, to you. Her ancestors were spotless Englishmen from the antiseptic island. There was only one case of vulgarity, and that was not their fault, obviously: one of her great-grandmothers committed the error of being an Indian. This lapse in taste was so well concealed that haughty Sylvia did not know about it until she was fully grown and ir-rev-o-cably possessed of moral virtue. She then conceived it as her duty to marry an Indian—fortunate fellow! Dr. Chowdhury is my husband's cousin, and that is how I know all about it."

Dorsey looked thoughtfully at the puffy, supercilious face, at the fugitive eyes, and then at the hands.

"Minna," said Dorsey, "you are tearing your handkerchief."

Minna started guiltily and hid her hands in the folds of her sari. "Perhaps I tear myself." The voice that had been so sneering and arrogant was now oddly choked. "I am neither discreet nor virtuous. I am very jealous. I am an evil woman."

"You make such a fuss about things," Dorsey said.

That night Dorsey's gaze wandered out across those unfathomable depths, up and up to the remote, pure, and inaccessible ends of the planet where, under a full moon, the Eternal Snows stood illumined, not by their own, but by an upper sea of light. The person she was carrying inside her stirred.

At that moment her maid came in, all smiles. "*Ma*," she said, "it is raining down below on the plains."

Joy

"A Tibetan lama came this morning," Dorsey said. "He was wearing a peaked cap and purple rags, like an exiled monarch. He sang the loveliest song—it went like this." She hummed it to Joy. "Only of course it didn't sound like that at all. And then do you know what he did? He cast grains of rice in the four directions—and all the while he was chanting prayers and blessing me in some fantastic language—I don't know if it was Sanskrit or Pali or Prakrit or what. Then he asked permission to sprinkle rice on my belly, and he was so nice that I let him. I imagine that was irregular, don't you? You know, there are yellow-ragged monks and purple-ragged monks, and the purple ones can get married."

Joy Davis Vora sniffled a little and blotted her blue eyes.

"Sorry," she said. "I haven't talked to Americans much lately. It took a lot of nerve for me to come to see you, but I figured you couldn't be very mean, in your condition."

"That shows how little you know about pregnancy," Dorsey said, trying to rearrange her weight in the chair, "but it's nice to hear your voice. You sound like—maybe Indiana."

"Terre Haute."

"I'm from San Francisco. You know, they'll never understand you here unless you waggle your head and talk very emphatically. You have to get your back into it. I'm working on this amazing accent—very highfalutin. They also like long, fancy words."

"It wasn't your accent there in the police station," Joy said. "It was when you laughed. I thought of it in the middle of the night."

"I thought I tittered," Dorsey grinned. "Then why were you afraid to come and see me?"

"I guess I wasn't, really. Just bewildered. But I wanted to talk to you, to ask your advice. Will you keep your American citizenship?"

"Certainly. Won't you?"

"I think they want to take it away from me."

"Why would they do that?"

Then the girl from Terre Haute told an intricate tale in which little things became big and big things became little, and finally they made a shape. A student in India, with very little money, she had lost both her money and her passport. An American woman named Mrs. Fraunhofer had taken a dislike to her, secretly accused her of being a spy for the Russians, and succeeded in getting the U.S. Government to delay granting her a new passport. Alone and broke in Calcutta, in the heat of summer, with dysentery, Joy had hit bottom. An Indian student—one with money, fortunately—had placed her with his family and provided her with medical care. When she was stronger, he sent her to Rampoche to recuperate. Just before she left, they were married.

"He'll come as soon as I send for him," Joy said.

"Better send for him, then," Dorsey said, gasping a little as she shifted her bulk over to one side. "Excuse me—this thing kicks. Tell you what: I'll help you raise hell over that passport business—later. It's just the sort of thing I'd like to do."

There were orchids from the forested slopes of Rampoche, and flowers that grew in gardens in England. The women had also brought objects believed to be useful to infants. Among other gifts on the table was a book from Minna Chakravarty: *The Sanskrit Infant Reader.*

Dorsey lay on the bed with the baby beside her. The women came in—Minna, Olga, Joy, Monica, and Sylvia—and hovered over them. For a long time they looked at the little homely creature. Monica said, "It isn't really so very dark," and she smiled up at Sylvia, who laughed. All of the women laughed, looking into one another's eyes—even Minna. Then they looked down and were quiet.

"Will you take him away to Paris, to New York?"

"No," Dorsey said, "I'll wait here."

The Sermon of the Flies

Roots came down out of the branches overhead, anchored themselves in the ground and became trees attached to other trees, and they were all one. An acre of banyan trees, an establishment of arches with leafy connections walking outward farther every year, it was a whole jungle in itself. Typical, thought Tino Scott, of the lack of definition in India. Lack of true individuality. Forms, concrete or abstract, never quite emerging as themselves, but interlacing, metamorphosing, compromising, agreeing before disagreement : . . .

For a moment he hesitated, standing there on the burning plain at two o'clock in the afternoon, full of anger.

A strident, otherworldly voice singing in slow, howling cadences, drew nearer, and the creaking of wooden axles rhythmically set the time. Out there in the sun two blue-black buffaloes were drawing a cart piled high with jute bags, on top of which rode the blue-black singer, a Santali tribesman, naked. Beside the buffaloes walked another black man, as in a dream. Behind them another cart with big wooden wheels, identical with the first, one man on top, one man walking. How slow, how very slow it all was, how large and massive, moving like some metaphysical demonstration without words, in the realm of aesthetic ideas having to do with time.

Either, Tino thought, I missed the argument which preceded it, and came in just as the Angel said, "See—*this* is what I mean"—

50

or I am the argument. Well, any fool could get the idea, but only a fool would try to state it.

Tearing off his dark glasses and the big peaked hat made of woven rushes, he stepped into the jungle. It was cooler there, but his flimsy Indian garments caught on the brambles, and immediately he stubbed his bare toe on a root.

He tucked his white cotton dhoti up around his waist, exposing long, well-defined legs with a certain amount of reddish hair on them; then he began cautiously to pick his way toward the center of the banyan, seeking, for no particular reason, the parent tree from which all these other root trees had sprung. It was dark in here, for the branches overhead interwove each other and were still more thickly joined together by vines and creepers.

A small cobra drew itself back suddenly into a nest of roots. Tino smiled grimly. He had assumed the presence of snakes; indeed, at this moment, he preferred them to certain other forms of life.

For instance, Mr. Wu Lu of the Chinese Department at Bharat University, where Tino taught, looked astonishingly like a toad. He was short, with a big hairless head and protruding eyes that were magnified into great opaque blurs by the thick lenses of his spectacles. But most of all it was his grin, spreading across his entire face, that made him look like a toad.

As a newcomer to the little Indian university, Tino had at first been filled with compassion for Wu Lu on account of this grin, considering it to be some hideous accident of nature, a congenital deformity or a psychophysical paralysis. It was too extreme and too steady to be mistaken for the Far Eastern grin of politeness, which may be arresting at times but is seldom actually unnerving.

This morning Tino had found out about Wu Lu's grin. Wu Lu was a Historical Force on the upswing; he was enjoying it, and, like History, he did not really care how he looked, for there were more important matters in the offing.

The quarrel had started, in a sense, over Janina the Polish girl.

She had been occupied first by the Nazis, then by the Russians; yet her foreign relations, because of her strange demeanor, remained somewhat enigmatic. Somehow she had escaped and made her way overland to India where, by courage and cunning, she was prolonging her stay through a series of scholarships at Indian universities.

Janina's mouth was pink and little, although her upper lip was habitually stiffened to conceal her long, dark teeth, and she was a bit saucer-eyed. However, her eyes were gray and she was a near blond and she had a suitable bust, and Tino was sure that, under her Indian sari in which she walked, barefoot, with a proper walk, all would be well, quite well. But she remained fiercely cerebral with him and was even a trifle waspish whenever he threatened to show a personal interest in her.

This morning, very early, she had startled him out of a sound sleep by pounding on the door of his hut. He appeared wrathfully before her, his suave, auburn hair a-strut, wearing only a lungi—a skirt-like garment hitched around the waist and falling to the ankles.

Nun-like, she kept her eyes fixed rigidly upon his face, although he gradually expanded his chest, of which he was proud, to present a more appreciable surface. She did not smile.

"Wu Lu babu has invited me to tea at ten o'clock," she said. "Kindly accompany me."

Tino mumbled fatuously.

"Good," Janina said. "I will meet you at the gate of Cheena Bhavan at ten-thirty." And she walked away.

Watching her depart, Tino was reminded that that was the stride that had taken her through Afghanistan—a stride that was firm but maidenly. Extraordinary, the whole thing. Doubtless, she was mysterious. "Like a banker," he said. "She has the face of a banker." As for the tea with Wu Lu, he supposed she had accepted because she could not afford to offend a professor, since she depended on scholarships for her existence. About her motive for asking him to accompany her, he could only speculate; but he was fairly sure that it was not altruism.

If Wu Lu was surprised to see Tino Scott, he did not show it. He was grotesquely jovial, bustling about to set out the tea things, forcing little cakes on his guests. The narrow but heavy shoulders and the thick neck suggested strength but not endurance—a kind of physical asperity, an impatience with any sustained effort, and yet a chemical propulsion toward effort.

They sat in the shade of a *krishnachura* tree on the cool west side of Wu Lu's house. The big fantastic flame-colored blossoms, shaped like orchids—"the crest of Krishna"—occasionally dropped about them.

It was not clear to Tino how they had got into the argument. From the weather they had gone on to the usual criticisms of India's "condition," which was, of course, a bad condition. There were the beggars lying about underfoot; there were the hundreds of thousands of mendicant holy men who wandered over the country, taking from the meager resources of the poor.

"And yet," Tino said, "Sisir babu assures me that the true India resides in these holy men, these sadhus."

"Sisir babu is a purveyor of opium for the masses," Wu Lu said in his staccato giggle to which Tino had tried in vain to become accustomed. "This religiosity! India exists in an opium dream. China has shaken it off."

Although he was tempted to defend dreams as over against a dreamless sleep, Tino merely said: "It's true, religion is the opium of some people. For others it is more like tobacco—it gives pleasure and poise. And smoke, the symbol of transitoriness, makes me reflect upon permanent values—doesn't it you? Of course, serious religion would be another matter." He offered Wu Lu a cigarette.

Wu Lu laughed politely and declined it.

"Tino babu is becoming Indianized," he said to Janina; and he went on to speak of the evils of the caste system, the persistence of child marriage, the abasement of women, corruption of officials, extremes of wealth and poverty, inefficiency, lack of organization, dirt and disease, starvation and cow worship. The only solution was for India to follow the example of China and Russia—break the chains, liberate the masses—

"Depends," said Tino, "on what you mean by liberation. Matter of Freedom. Can't be free in a belly-centered country, you know. India needs her Brahmans. But make every man a Brahman, eh?—responsible for the country."

Wu Lu said through his maddening grin: "India is decadent. Culturally it has nothing to lose. That is because its controlling ideas have not sprung from the people. Or if they did originate in the healthy life of the masses, they were seized by the priesthood and the business interests and turned against the masses in order to enslave them."

Janina was drinking cups of tea and cramming sweet biscuits into her mouth, taking care to keep her upper lip stretched chastely down over those questionable teeth. The lower part of her face chewed vigorously while the upper part kept austere vigil. All at once she closed her big round gray eyes, gulped, opened them, and said:

"From Wu Lu babu's point of view, communism has to do with agrarian reform. From Tino babu's point of view, it means the police state. It is a matter of semantics."

"Excuse me"—Wu Lu giggled—"but it is hardly worth arguing about. It is not a moral question, but the inescapable movement of History."

Tino looked at him curiously. At this moment the professor appeared to him like a trick of the mind, a sophism with mutually dependent parts, impenetrable on its own terms, hostile to the employment of other terms. In vain he searched the magnified eyes for some sign of personal weakness; there was no weakness because there was somehow no person, but only a kind of abstract relationship of symbols for quantity.

"It is a moral question," Tino said, "because of the choice one makes: whether to join this particular movement or to defend oneself against it. Communists are like the priests who pretend to know the future. By their melodramatic air" (he nearly said paranoid grin) "they can exploit the gullible. They merely make other people angry. This is the inescapable movement of History —back and forth."

Tino felt, all at once, that he had gone too far. The few foreigners who were at the university were indispensable to one another's social life; for the caste- and race-conscious Hindus were obliged to guard their homes—containing perhaps no more than two or three rooms—lest their ladies be exposed to the casual view of outsiders, or some of the many ritual observances be trampled ignorantly underfoot. Among this handful of foreigners—Europeans and Asiatics—there existed a diversity of opinion fully as great as that of the nations they came from. Indeed, these individuals, taken out of context, as it were, represented their national interests with far greater clarity and intensity, and only with less power, than did the nations themselves. They did it involuntarily for the most part, for they did not look upon themselves as representative but rather as marginal persons, rootless and unassimilated, for one reason or another, in the societies they had left; yet, in a strange land, feeling their own identity endangered, they summoned up in themselves more strongly than ever the very cultural traits against which they had formerly rebelled. This was tacitly understood and respected. It was also understood that no one could stand alone for long and maintain his humanity. To preserve the common bond, there existed a kind of gentleman's agreement among these foreigners not to take sides too openly or too vigorously in the great political issues. Yet here were Tino Scott and Wu Lu on the brink of war. Tino felt he must, at all costs, rise above the clumsy dualism of the argument—and he was getting precious little help from Janina— somehow to bring out the good old common bond.

"Back and forth," Tino said. "Through our impatience we have made great progress. Because of our impatience we are unable to enjoy our progress."

Janina popped a biscuit into her mouth, splashed tea after it, glugged, and said, "Perhaps progress is a difficult thing to enjoy in any case."

"For India, impossible," Wu Lu said. "Her population increases by five millions every year—soon it will be ten millions, fifteen millions. A radical change is needed, a new world. Only communism can answer the need of India."

Tino said: "If all of India's resources, material, cultural, spiritual, were scientifically organized and devoted exclusively to the problem of filling India's belly, I grant you, it might succeed in doing just that—and no more—for about fifty years. After that, you will be confronted by a greatly enlarged digestive tract which can only live by devouring other digestive tracts. It may have got rid of capital, but it will also be devoid of interest. Or do I seem uncooperative?"

Janina nodded her head vigorously.

"It will not be America who organizes India," Wu Lu said. "All the world knows that she would destroy India, if she could, just as she has tried to destroy Korea and China by germ warfare."

Tino closed his eyes. The repetition of this charge, even by apparently disinterested people, was having a more and more abrasive effect upon his temper. At first his rebuttals had been calm, clear, and impeccably logical. Now he felt himself lucky if he could keep from hurling insults. It was the repetition, the confounded repetition!

A still more fixed look had come over the grin-gashed face of Mr. Wu Lu. It shone, as it were, with a light not its own, as the Voice of History rattled forth compulsively:

"The treachery of America is well known, but the warmongers will be crushed. America will be driven out of Asia. China, not

America, will dominate Asia. She will dominate Europe—and America also. She will crush America. . . ." The Voice of History stopped to giggle.

Two small brown wrens went bouncing unafraid through the company, hunting for building material. With straws and fibers crammed in their bills crosswise, they looked like little stiff-whiskered tigers. A scarlet hummingbird hung for a long time over a bed of ranunculi before departing. It had been unable to decide about a black bee that clung in a period of concentration, dead, its sting piercing a smooth scarlet petal.

Tino said quietly, "Mr. Wu Lu."

"Yes."

"We are tired of germs."

"Then you should stop using them against the People's Republic of China."

"We were merely amusing ourselves for a little while. We have now perfected the Cosmic Bomb. With one Bomb we are going to wipe China off the map. This will take place next Thursday at two o'clock in the afternoon. Don't tell anyone. It would just worry people needlessly."

Wu Lu was petrified. He was gray in color. His mouth hung down like a rubber bag.

As they walked away, Janina remarked: "I was glad you have said it. And I have said nothing."

Tino was not glad. It meant open warfare at the university, with himself as the probable loser.

Had he come here as a sort of professional American, with an ax to grind, he might have welcomed the break with some gusto. But he had come quite on his own, to learn Sanskrit, to teach Western languages, and above all to live—to live with still others of his fellow inhabitants of the global country in which he had been born. And now, in the twitch of a nerve, here he was, a foreign invader defending an invisible outpost of his clan. It had been his intention to defend, if anything, India—horrible, hopeless, magnificent India which he loved with the unrequited love of an outcaste patriot. And even that—well, it was all muddled now; or perhaps it was that an agreeable dream was breaking up and the reality was too clear, too sharp for comfort.

It had begun innocently enough. The vice chancellor simply had suggested that it might be nice if Tino would give a series of public lectures on the great writers of the West, from Homer up to the time when Western Literature was superseded by Rabindranath Tagore. Each of these lectures was accompanied by a tree-planting ceremony with songs and dances. There were a Homer Tree and a Virgil Tree, a Dante Tree and a Goethe Tree, and so on. He had wondered about the propriety of a T. S. Eliot Tree—for he had insisted on talking about "modern" literature—and was greatly relieved when they merely served biscuits.

As a result of these lectures he had come to be regarded as an apologist for the West; and indeed it was hard for him to remain impartial in the face of attacks—often quite devious—by both communists and Indian nationalists. At first, in order to advance "the truth" within the generous universe of discourse, he generally supported what was being attacked and attacked what was being supported, then, by reconciling the opposites, he attempted to show that a new and helpful position had been reached by both sides.

Little by little, however, he found himself accepting the karma of an American partisan: a position that would not otherwise have been represented here. And now, now that he had threatened Wu Lu with a Cosmic Bomb, it would be a dogfight. Gone were his modest hopes of Promoting Understanding, blasted was his Bridge Between East and West.

Tino came upon a little clearing in the middle of the banyan jungle. A patch of blue sky showed overhead. In the clearing stood the parent tree, an ancient stump about ten feet high, dead

and quite detached from the surrounding structure of trees that
had once stemmed from it.

A naked brown man, about Tino's own age, sat cross-legged in
the shadow at the base of the dead tree. His long, matted hair
was bleached reddish brown by exposure to sun and rain. Mark-
ings of sandalwood paste were on his forehead. Although he was
smiling slightly, there had been no change of expression, no sign
of surprise. Indeed, he was not looking directly at Tino. The
great dark liquid eyes, set wide apart under a broad forehead,
gazed like those of a forest creature at the first perceived dawn
of the world; gazed, but with an antiquity of lively intelligence,
at the World as Spectacle.

It was the Recurrent Face which appeared perhaps once or
twice, perhaps not at all, during a moment of peculiar sensitivity
out of all the slow, fluctuating eons of an ancient civilization.
Tino had known it once in Japan, in the face of a Zen Buddhist,
and in sculpture once at Angkor Vat—not the hundreds of ap-
proximations, but the One that stood apart, revealed by an impossible chance of genius—perhaps once at Sarnath, and repeated a
dozen times at Ajanta—the face of the Illumined Buddha. Standing
on the desert, in the shade of a boulder, not far from the caves
of Ajanta, he had kicked up a piece of carved stone that spoke
directly to something more than his understanding, surmounting
barriers of time and idiom. It was the merest fragment of the Face
—part of the mouth and cheek; and yet it was all there, in *omnibus
partibus*, the Whole. It was one with the stone Buddhas in that
cave farther up the hill. The setting sun shone into the cave
mouth to reveal them, illumined as by an inner light, looking out
—and in—on the world of mankind with ultimate human wisdom,
with infinite compassion, and with a very subtle touch of irony.

Slowly the great elongated eyes moved and looked into the
dark, troubled eyes of the stranger, where they saw—more than
the stranger. They did not look away. There was no greeting between the two, for it was as if there had never been a time when

they had not been together. Tino approached and sat down opposite this Person. No word was spoken.

Almost immediately the tense face of the white man relaxed, and then it began, by almost imperceptible degrees, to mirror the inward slight smile, at once abstract and personal, of the brown man.

On the ground beside this sadhu or holy man was a glass tumbler from which he had drunk tea—evidently someone had brought it to him from a nearby hut or village, for there were no signs of preparations here. A dozen flies were buzzing around the tumbler; several were down inside, eating the sugar.

The sadhu's eyes shifted ever so slightly from Tino's eyes to the tumbler, then back again, without disturbing their strange rapport. Deliberately the brown hand reached out; with a sudden movement it turned the tumbler upside down, trapping three flies inside, and withdrew. The flies buzzed frantically behind the glass walls of their prison.

Seeing that Tino had understood, the sadhu reached out again with the same slow, deliberate gesture, and turned the tumbler back to its original position. The three flies fled out into the wide world.

Tino's pulse was quick. He realized that he was extraordinarily happy, although it seemed unlikely that he would ever be so again. It would not do to wait. He stood up and backed away, still gazing like a receding mirror into that face. He groped in the deep pockets of his long Punjabi shirt, for some gift he could leave. First, there was money, but he would be ashamed to offer that. There was a small pocket compass—to set the man on his way? And there was his wrist watch—a useful gift, no doubt! He could not give any of these things.

At the edge of the little clearing was a bush covered with small white five-petaled *champa* flowers that would give out their sweet odor at dusk. Tino started to pick one, to offer it, and yet he was suddenly reluctant to do even that small violence to the bush. And when he thought of taking one that had already fallen to the ground, that hardly seemed right either. No, all this was irrelevant. No exchange was possible. It would be merely to move an object about as if in play.

But the perfect gesture, it must be made. Not the *namaskar*, the clasped hands and the bow of salutation, for that was indicative of a beginning and an ending, when there was no beginning and no ending.

In despair Tino stood and looked at the sadhu. Then he knew that this man had need of nothing. Once again he paused, smiled into the sadhu's eyes, seeing his own image there. Gently he turned and stepped into the jungle.

As he walked over the burning plain toward the university, the sun hurt his eyes. He fumbled for his dark glasses. Before putting them on, he cupped them in his hand, held them up, and used them as a mirror, but he was not quick enough. What he saw was a slightly foolish mask.

"Life is generally fatal," Peter Bruff said without a trace of humor. "Only—a few of us die too suddenly, leaving obligations so pressing that we must return to fulfill them."

The subject caused me a degree of uneasiness which Peter evidently construed as disagreement.

"Among those present," he insisted, "are those who are too discreet to show themselves, for they exist in a different modality. If there is sufficient reason, they will appear; but it sets a dangerous precedent."

We were sitting on the veranda of his bungalow, drinking chang out of big sections of bamboo with copper bands around them. The place was Kalimpong, a mountain town in North India, surrounded by Nepal, Sikkim, and Tibet. Of Peter Bruff I knew very little, except that he bought and sold Tibetan art objects. We had met in a Calcutta bar, and he had asked me up for the summer, simply. I had accepted partly because I liked him, but mainly in order to escape the heat of the Bengal plains, where I had been teaching English at Bharat University.

That morning I had seen the whole Himalayan Range spread out before a massive, slow dawn. In the mountain barrier, carved in golden snow against a flaming sky, there lay a U-shaped pass, called Nalanda. From very early times, caravans had made their way by that pass, into Tibet and China, and back into India, bringing goods and evils and states of consciousness. Even now, at dusk, in the caravanserai down the mountain from us, a mule train prepared to leave.

Peter Bruff lit his pipe. The match flame flickered before a young, malaria-ravaged face that was handsome in an austere way. At twenty-four, his gray eyes were those of a boy who has seen too many unseasonable events. Several times Peter leaned forward as if he were about to speak, but each time he was prevented by some inner scruple. The reason for this became apparent when he finally did begin to speak. He had been born a Philadelphia Quaker and he would always be one, regardless of what else he became; he did not like to show emotion; and the story he told —which evidently affected him deeply—cost him many an un-Quakerly silence.

I have not told this to anyone before (Peter Bruff said), but I should like to tell it now—not so much to bear out the statements I made to you, but as a confession and a tribute to someone who has meant a great deal to me.

When I first came to India I stayed at Benares Hindu University with Boris Wing, a friend of mine from San Francisco. In the same house where we lived was an extraordinarily learned young Brahman named Ananda Mahadev, who often helped Boris through the intricacies of Indian philosophy. Ananda was sitting cross-legged on a mat in his room, with—incongruously—a type-writer before him, when I first saw him. Enormous dark eyes that seemed to have a light in them glanced up at me and through me. The light-brown face, with its delicate bone structure, was both subtle and strong. Evidently he had just had his bath, as he was freshly oiled and wearing a kind of hand towel. The sacred thread of the Brahman caste hung from his shoulder. This tall, well-formed man leaped to his feet and with great courtesy invited us in. We sat with him while he expounded a problem in Sankara's philosophy to Boris, who listened with his head on one side, his boyish, Chinese-American face very attentive. I was more aware of Ananda's whole personality—his dignity and kindness, his rich and enlightened humanity—than of his brilliant exposition of the problem.

Where Ananda found the time to devote to me, I shall never know, for he was hard at work on his doctoral dissertation. But he wandered with me all over Benares, that oldest of living cities. Sometimes Boris accompanied us, but most often Ananda and I walked alone; and as we walked we discoursed on the things of heaven and earth, the nature of reality, the destiny of man. . . .

Through that ancient hive of civilization we roamed, exploring winding streets so narrow that in places one can touch the walls on both sides at once. Against these walls we squeezed to let the goddess Kali pass in the form of humped milky-white cattle with long, dark, knowing eyes, who seemed to have reached that state of detachment for which mystics strive. Beggars and wandering monks, pilgrims and prostitutes, scholars, merchants, coolies, anonymous hordes milled about with a vitality that filled me with an obscure restlessness. And they chewed pan, a savory leaf containing betel nut and lime and sugar, and when they spat it was as crimson as a stream of blood. It was the world, the swarming world. Yet, as we walked down by the vast river which Indians call Ganga Mata—Mother Ganges—River of Life, we seemed to be walking along the boundary of another world, thinly veiled from us by the veil of Maya. There by the burning-ghats we watched priests burning the bodies of the dead and casting the ashes upon the Holy River. It is the City of the Dead, to which multitudes of pious Hindus, with failing strength, hasten on their last pilgrimage; for here Ganga Mata has power to grant the soul a long sleep before another incarnation; and indeed, on Ganga Mata, Nirvana itself is very near.

As we stood beside a river temple, watching the smoke curl up from the funeral pyres, and the little boats taking the ashes out on the river, I said: "Everyone succeeds in dying. Nobody fails."

"We Hindus are relativists," said Ananda. "We are the accumulation of lives that have gone before, the premonition of lives to be lived. And do you not feel that all this is simultaneous—Now? We prepare for life beyond, and it is 'beyond' in that it is achieved by piercing deeply through the vanities of this market place, into the timeless reality. The beyond is achieved and lost, perhaps daily; but it is always there—and here within—for Ganga Mata is wherever you are."

I asked him ironically if he thought all was vanity, and he said, with his serious smile: "All is not vanity, but it is absolutely necessary to think so at certain times. If Death thought we valued life, he would make things much more difficult for us."

"You're really not serious, Ananda," I said. "How can you live with so many gods? India is so crowded anyway."

"God has many aspects," he said.

I told him I was an agnostic.

"I too," he said. "And I too shall make the journey on Ganga Mata. God is also in my disbelief."

A religious festival was in progress during my last three nights in Benares. Processions of priests and multitudes of devotees swarmed through the city, bearing flower-decked images of Shiva the Destroyer in his phallic form, symbol of joy and renewal. They were a living unity, to which I was a foreign particle. They flowed around me. I withdrew into myself.

Just before dawn, I went down to the river with Ananda to watch him at his ritual bathing and yoga exercises. He wanted me to come into the water, which was more than liberal of him, since it is, after all, holy water. I stood on the bank and looked at the muddy river, swollen by the monsoon rains. It swirled dangerously. I felt a little ashamed of myself, as I was sure I could swim better than Ananda, yet there he was in the water, beckoning me. I think the thing that kept me back was the fact that the water was really liquid mud—and we were just downstream from the burning-ghats. I wouldn't have relished a mouthful of ashes, no matter how sanctified they were. Mud, perhaps, but not ashes.

After his bath he sat on the river bank, cross-legged, in the padmasana, or lotus posture, and chanted Sanskrit prayers from the Vedas: noble and lofty architecture of poetry. And when he came to the final *om*, the sacred syllable of peace, I felt thoroughly at peace. But after a time, as I watched Ananda's face, I exclaimed at the complexity I found there:

"Ananda, with all your knowledge, you are not happy! You who sit here possess the secret power of happiness. Then why not use it?"

"It is a dreadful force," he replied somberly, "which I fear to let loose, lest it destroy me and the world."

"Really, I don't understand."

"I am using my knowledge, do not fear. By not using it I am using it—the Mystic Union is like the hydrogen bomb. After it there is no experience, only desolation. I am—humanity is—made of experience, fighting, and suffering. Not through me shall we ever dehumanize ourselves. Not through me shall the war come to an end, for its end will be the end of Man. But you, Peter"— he smiled at me across oceans of time, with the delicate and compassionate irony of Buddha, who so loved man that he lived long—"you may come to me some night and find me seated like this, my gaze indrawn, and you will not know me. And indeed my tormented self will have ceased to exist. In its place will be that Other, the Great Self. Then sit thou and pay attention; but beware, for thou shalt be in the sacred presence of Happiness itself."

On leaving Benares, I continued my journey through India, and for a whole year I traveled restlessly from one place to another, seeking the answer to the great unformulated question that is my life. For some time I was in a Buddhist monastery in Ceylon, meditating on the prospects of purity in the mystical sense, that "emptying the self of the self" to make room for the Divine. It seemed to me an admirable way of life, and not wholly unattainable. With me it was a problem of commitment. I would have considered it a species of ingratitude to have abandoned my guiding principle, that mediocrity which has created my character —too weak for anything but change, too sensual to resist education—and which has taught me to revere all extravagances of the human spirit. Purification by nonachievement is my way. *Je suis mystique, et au fond je ne crois à rien.*

In my ignorance I had supposed that I would find more than one person like Ananda in India. It took me a year to realize that there was no one in the world like him. I traveled the length of the country, back to Benares, to find Ananda once again. And, like a good Hindu going there to die, the closer I got to Holy Benares, the more contented I became.

Ananda was not at his lodgings. Boris Wing was away, and I could find none of the students who had known them. The university offices had closed for the day. I wandered alone through the darkening city, along the paths Ananda and I had followed, hoping that I would meet him. Night fell, and I was extremely depressed, although a great religious festival was in progress, as at this same time the previous year.

As I walked along a dark, winding alley, a door opened to my left, several feet from the ground. A squat figure stood framed in the doorway, silhouetted against a flickering oil lamp somewhere within. He was a so-called holy man, stark naked, with long, matted hair, and he was smeared from head to foot with bluish ashes. Streamers of smoke curled slowly past him from the interior of the room, where I could see other holy men sitting on the floor, smoking hashish. They all had dreamy, vacuous expressions on their faces—having reached, without the tiresome discipline of yoga, a state of abstraction which made them feel that they had loosened the bonds of "this world." Even in their exalted state, they were not insensitive to money. They permitted me to join them. After all, they felt, a certain license ought to prevail during a religious festival.

When I emerged, after some time, I had the sensation that I was moving along about a foot and a half above the ground, gliding rather than walking. In Chowkhambha, the market place, I floated like a wraith among the dark, festive multitude. A white face appeared before me—an albino Indian who looked strangely like me. I was unsure of my own identity on that disquieting night as I lost my way, penetrating deeper and deeper into the ahistorical, coming, at bottom, to the Golden Temple and its eternally thrusting Shiva from which flowed all life. The strangenesses and the wetnesses of other bodies, other souls, out of other ages and planets and states of being, streamed past me and around me, engulfing me. It was like some blind, autonomic process of the body on the inside—digestion and excretion, menstruation, parturition. And gradually I was being drawn *inside* with that submissive horde who went so fluidly, so "subjectively," so unproblematically. Something deep in my bones was scandalized, feeling itself near death in that life of the Womb.

At that moment, in the midst of the human sea, I saw Ananda. And at the same time he saw me. In our delight we rushed at each other and embraced in the Indian manner. I cannot tell you how moved I was—and he also. My spirits soared. . . . We did not speak for some time, but walked toward the outskirts of the city. The sky was still dark; but far away, beyond the second great bend in the river, I could detect the faintest sign of dawn. We came to Ganga Mata.

"Why have you brought me here?" Ananda asked, and his face was troubled. I jostled him playfully.

"Last year you wanted me to go in with you," I said, "and I wouldn't—not because I felt too unclean for Ganga Mata, but because I thought Ganga Mata was too unclean for me. Now we are going in."

Ananda stood on the bank, wrapped in his white Kashmiri chuddar, and gazed out over the waters. "Not now," he murmured. "See how turbulent she is."

I laughed, and began to strip off my clothes.

"You will go in?" he asked sadly.

"I will go in."

Slowly he began to undress. I waited for him, and at length we stood naked, poised on the bank, watching the dark, violent waters swirling below us. Ananda said something I did not catch. It sounded like "return." I looked at him, and he seemed to me, at that moment, like one of his own Vedic gods. I started to dive in, to be there when he came, in case the current was too strong for him. He stopped me. Looking into my eyes, and pointing down at the water, he said:

"Man is created out of black turmoil, out of the Chaos of the unconscious—out of nothing. Is it any wonder that he should be prone to negation, sin, and vulgar anxiety—to an inherent neurasthenia—since his dominant memory is of Chaos. What can lure him out of fear, but love and faith in love?"

"Love and faith take courage," I said, "and man is cowardly."

"The ultimate courage does not rest in man," said Ananda. "Man is full of quibbling trepidations which only Shiva, the real Man, can allay—the Lord of Thunder, the Hero whose flaming sword vanquishes Eternal Night." He descended into the water.

I was there before him, cutting the water with a clean dive; but I went too deep and too far. Eddies and whirlpools sucked me under. I swallowed water and mud; the current carried me far out; I exhausted myself fighting merely to stay afloat in that torrent. It seemed to me that I was underwater most of the time. My struggles were growing weaker, and I was beginning to lose consciousness, when I became aware that Ananda had me by the hair and was holding my face above water. Slowly he was drawing me to the bank, far downstream.

When we reached shore, I was half unconscious. I lay on the

cold, muddy bank. Soon my whole being was suffused by a delicious warmth, and I knew vaguely that Ananda was covering me with his beautiful white chuddar. I must have protested feebly at first, for I seem to remember his placing his hand on my head, and he said something like this, just before I lapsed into an exhausted sleep:

"My life has been a preparation for this moment in which I meet you. This is my great climax, the time of the fulfillment of my history. But who are you? You are anyone, it does not matter who. In this meeting I am fully realized. There is no need for a future, any more than there is a need for a separate identity. All things converge here, now, at this point of union between thee and me: the birds reaching the goal of the evolution of flight, the sun of his career and the moon of hers, sky, stars, bridge, time, space, and destiny—all have worked toward our meeting which contains their whole purpose and significance. We, here, now, this, are the *telos*. And what do I say to thee? I say: 'Good morning,' and thou sayest to me: 'Good morning,' and we pass each other, and all things are satisfied."

When I awoke, the dawn was full, and I was surrounded by a group of holy men who had come down to the river for their ritual ablutions. I was naked except for Ananda's white chuddar. Ananda was nowhere to be seen. The holy men did not know him. I made my way back to my room near the university, bathed, and had breakfast, expecting Ananda to arrive at any moment. Before long I heard footsteps, and leaped up to greet— Boris Wing.

"Pete!" he yelled, pounding me. "Where have you been? Why didn't you write? I was worried about you."

I apologized, and tried to explain that I had been in rather a poor condition, only dreamily aware of the passage of time, and unable to bring myself to write to anyone at all. Then I told him of my dawn adventure with Ananda, and showed him the white chuddar, all stained with mud.

Boris's eyes grew wide, then filled with tears. He put his hand on my shoulder, and said quietly:

"Peter, I have to tell you this. Ananda was drowned in the river—a year ago today."

The body had not been recovered. I burned the white chuddar on the riverbank, and cast the ashes into Ganga Mata.

Out of the caravanserai down the mountain from Peter Bruff's bungalow, the mule train was starting on its long and perilous trip to Lhasa. One by one the laden beasts, ghostly in the moonlight, passed along the trail, although I could see no mule driver.

I asked no questions; for I shared with Peter Bruff a strange, secret, and improbable courtesy that lay, as Ananda said, "also in my disbelief." Those who tease God learn not to speak first.

◀◖◇◖◇◖◇◖◇◖◇◖◀◖ *The Touchable*

     We pedaled on across a semiarid plain with rice paddies in the low places and villages in the high places: a cluster of mud huts with thatched roofs that seemed to rise effortlessly out of the landscape and were in perfect harmony with it; a pond that was at once the community water supply, public bath, and laundry—with hyacinths and lilies and sometimes lotuses growing in it; parrots in the coconut trees and the date palms; gray-vested crows everywhere; tiny black goats with a preference for dried cow dung; pale cows with humps on their backs; and perched on these cows, or prospecting about them like common chickens, were white herons, fantastically elegant.

Each village had strict zoning ordinances, unwritten, according to caste. The Brahmans lived in one section; they were, in general, the color of coffee with cream, and they took their ease, for the world was their oyster. The next castes down, with smaller and smaller amounts of sacred cream in their coffee—although there was some variety, always duly noted, commented on, and evaluated—inhabited the central and less desirable sections of the village. On the outskirts of the village, resigned to coffee without cream and to life without status—for they were not permitted to approach the temple or even to allow their shadow to touch the shadow of a servant of a Hindu—were the Untouchables. They had to have their own, separate mud puddle.

My companion was Aretino Scott—Tino—the handsome, dark-eyed, auburn-haired American who taught at Bharat University. As the district was familiar to Tino, and it was a clement time of year—September—he had offered to show me the countryside of this part of Bengal. By two o'clock in the afternoon we had finished off the bottle of boiled water we had brought with us; and although there was plenty of water in the village ponds, it was guaranteed to reduce our life expectancy: in our thirties, we were already far beyond the average age for India. I suggested that we stop in the next village for tea, since people generally boiled the water when they made tea. "Yes," Tino chuckled, "and they wash the cups in the nearest buffalo wallow!" However, he said, if I could hold out for another half-hour, we should come to a small town with a tea shop where he had connections.

The town we were headed for turned out to be considerably more than half an hour away. By the time we got there, I was quite peevish. Tino was wearing an ironic smile, which was apparently uncontrollable, since I had already given him several black looks. I thought he was amused at my discomfiture. So I was not at all happy when we descended at a little open-air tea shop and the proprietor rushed out, made a dive at Tino's feet, touched the top of his shoes and then the top of his own head. Tino's efforts to prevent this abasement were quite halfhearted. In fact, he appeared disgustingly happy.

Two jolly-looking lads placed a table and benches for us in the shade of a mango tree, at a distance from the other customers —for they were Brahmans with sacred threads over their sacred left shoulders and sacred locks of hair looped up in back, and they would feel contaminated by the likes of us. Out of a locked box the proprietor produced special cups and saucers, thus reassuring, not us, but the Brahmans: beef-eating lips would not touch *their* cups, anyway. In such a place even the sight of an untouchable would have been intolerable to them. I was not pleased with India at that moment.

Over the tea and the many tidbits which the proprietor served

us in person, I let Tino know that I disapproved of the foot
dusting he had allowed himself to receive—even though I knew
it was an Indian custom. It seemed to me, I said, that these were
a gentle though vicious people, and too easy to take advantage of
because of their belief in nonviolence. Tino's ironic smile broad-
ened into a grin, and then at last he gave me the apology and the
explanation for which I had been longing. "I see that I must tell
you a little story," he said, "because I have been rude. Since the
source of my rudeness is discretion, I shall now be indiscreet. In
return, you must promise that you will be discreet about it."

As I was already quite mollified, I made the promise, and I
hope to keep it.

"At three o'clock in the afternoon," Tino Scott said, "on
August 1, 1952, I was careening along at breakneck speed through
Calcutta traffic, in a rickety bus driven by a bearded Sikh in a
turban. Narrowly missing rickshaws, oxcarts, bicycles, pedes-
trians, trams, and flivvers, we were approaching Putiary Station,
one of the old districts where Westerners are seldom seen. The
bus was not just packed; it overflowed. Men clustered like swarms
of bees around the front and back openings, clinging for dear
life when we rounded corners. An official notice in back of the
driver's seat said: 'Maximum capacity 30 Passengers.' I estimated
that there were at least sixty-five passengers. I, the only non-
Indian, was hanging by one hand from a metal rod suspended
from the ceiling—there was no room for my other hand. Bodies
were crammed against me fore and aft. It was impossible to fall,
even if I had died suddenly. I swayed when they swayed, tottered when they tottered, and I waited to be disgorged at the
next stop.

"Plastered against my forward surface was the thin, elegant
backbone of Arjuna babu, my good friend who had come with
me from Bharat University, a hundred miles away by train. An
unseen person, himself under pressure from behind, fitted moistly

over my entire southern surface. Arjuna twisted his neck around, looked soulfully at me, and gave his head a wry flirt which meant, in Bengali, that we were nearly there, such as we were.

"Suddenly the brakes squawked, the bus flung itself to a halt, the wooden structure in which we were riding leaned forward, and everyone hurtled into the front of the bus in a wild tangle of bodies. The front door opened and they began to fall out—on their feet, surprisingly—into a large mud puddle. The unseen person behind me slithered around me and began forcing his way through the door.

"On a vague impulse I felt for my wallet, which I kept in my hip pocket. It was gone. Leaping down the steps, I seized the end of a blue Punjabi shirttail just as it was disappearing into the crowd. Pulling it in, hand over hand, I found myself confronted by a short, swarthy youth who was glaring at me with an expression of outraged dignity.

" 'What is the meaning of this?' he demanded in Bengali.

" 'I think you picked my pocket,' I said.

" 'Very well, search me!' he cried contemptuously. 'Search me!' My confidence was vanishing, but I searched him nevertheless, going through all the pockets in his long, blue Punjabi shirt which hung down over his dhoti. Lifting it up, I considered this latter garment: some six yards of white cotton cloth wound loosely around the upper legs and knotted about the waist. Blue Boy sneered. 'Well, Sahib?' After all!

"I was about to begin my apologies, when Arjuna dashed up. 'What happened?'

" 'My pocket was picked, but—' That was all Arjuna needed. His fist shot out and caught the youth a resounding blow on the jaw. Blue Boy staggered, and my wallet promptly dropped out of the inner recesses of his dhoti into the mud. I picked it up.

"At least a hundred men were looking on by this time. They made a tight ring around Arjuna, the pickpocket, and me. They began to mutter, then to shout. 'What are they saying, Arjuna?'

" 'They are going to stone him to death,' Arjuna replied. 'He has brought shame on them before a foreigner.'

"Blue Boy was trembling violently. His eyes darted this way and that, looking for a way of escape. There was none. A hundred or more self-appointed executioners had suddenly surrounded him and were staring at him with hatred.

" 'Look here!' I called out to the grim mob around us. 'I got my wallet back. I'm satisfied.' They did not budge. 'It was my fault.' I said. 'I put temptation in his way. It was in my hip pocket. All wrong, see?' They did not see. They had begun to equip themselves with rocks. Two men laid hold of the thief. I pushed them off, grasped Blue Boy by the hand and began to pump it ostentatiously. 'Hey!' I yelled. 'Forgive those who do you evil!' I sermonized further. It fell on stony soil. Again they laid hold of him, but they were lacking in resolution, perhaps because they unconsciously associated me with the old British overlords, but also, I like to think, because I had my left arm possessively around Blue Boy's neck, and my right fist, raised high in a theatrical gesture, was ready to descend violently on somebody —and Bengalis are small men with delicate bones.

" 'You criticize America for her lynchings—which are ancient history,' I said. 'Now you're going to lynch this boy!'

"This time they yelled back at me furiously: 'No, no! Not lynch! We *stone* him! Stand back!'

"Still clutching my man, I pushed slowly toward a little roadside tea shop, arguing meanwhile. 'Lynch or stone—same thing—without due process of law—jury of his peers! You're just a lynch mob—disgrace to India—worse than pickpockets!' Instead of shaming them, I merely infuriated them. They howled anti-American slogans at me. By this time, however, I had reached the tea shop. Dragging Blue Boy by the arm, I shoved him down on a bench against the wall, wedged myself against him, and pulled a broad table up against our ribs. Arjuna sat on the other side of me. Across this table we three contemplated the angry mob, which shuffled and glared at us from a distance of four feet.

"I ordered tea. Never before had I had such an opportunity of playing the hero without much direct danger to myself, and I enjoyed it to the full. It was simply wonderful. I knew that I was absolutely right, for once, that I was actually dominating a situation and that I could win. With the calm of Walter Mitty, I contemplated my next move. Arjuna was numb and speechless, but loyal to me. The pickpocket stared blackly at the table—he was in the stocks. The mob stirred impatiently. I thought of sending Arjuna for the police, but I was afraid the mob would not let him through, for he was a Bengali like themselves—I was the only unknown quantity. If Arjuna tried and failed, it would add perilously to their sense of power. There must be no failures at this point. I sipped tea. Arjuna sipped tea. Blue Boy sat like a stone, jammed between me and the wall.

"Across from the tea shop was a corner around which two sets of tram rails curved. On the nearest one sat an empty tram. Every few minutes a tram came along, stopped on the other side of the empty one, just even with it, and continued on its way. One was approaching now.

"Pulling Blue Boy with me, I stood up with an exalted expression, as if I were about to make a great speech—and Bengalis cannot resist speeches. Pointing to Heaven, I marched with measured steps straight at the crowd, which opened to permit my demonstration. I did not have to hold onto Blue Boy—he was leaning against me like a Siamese twin, mechanically keeping step with me. The mob was puzzled. We were marching like a doomed man and his priest to the scaffold. Only, it was not a scaffold—it was the empty tram—and we were actually climbing into it before they realized that they were being tricked. As the leaders swarmed in after me, I pushed Blue Boy through the door on the other side, into the tram which had just arrived, and turned to confront them.

" 'Shame on you!' I said, bracing myself firmly in the doorway.

Looking over my shoulder, I saw Blue Boy walk up to the front of his car, sit down primly in back of the conductor, and stare fixedly ahead of him, as if by concentrating he could make the vehicle move.

"It did move. And I had the leaders of the mob in my empty tram, unable to go forward through me or to go back through their followers. The other tram was some distance down the tracks, and gaining speed, before the mob outside quite grasped the situation. They dropped their rocks. Leaning backward through the doorway, I glimpsed the dapper blue shirt of the pickpocket as his tram rounded another corner. I began to laugh.

"Arjuna and I started walking toward Banarjipara Road where his friend Biren lived. A group of young men followed us. I turned and faced them. They told me that they had observed everything and were heartily ashamed of their countrymen. 'Fine,' I said. They told me I had taught them a lesson. I said I doubted it. They hoped I would not carry away a bad impression of India. I said India was a big place, that I had many impressions, some good, some bad, and that they should be less concerned with impressions and more concerned with their *dharma*—which means doing your duty. (Arjuna told me, much later, during some heated words, that I had embarrassed him at this point by what he called my 'cynical self-righteousness.' But it is so hard to stop being a hero!)

"At Biren's house that night there was a slight difficulty about sleeping arrangements. Biren had two mosquito curtains: one big one and one little one. The big one had most of one side missing, while the little one had only a few medium-sized holes. Although I protested against preferential treatment, they insisted that I take the little one and sleep on the wooden platform by the window, while they slept on the floor, under the big curtain. I was too tired to argue long.

"Arjuna and Biren were snoring gently in unison, and I was playing games with mosquitoes, when a head appeared suddenly at the barred, moonlit window beside my bed. An arm in a blue sleeve darted between the bars, poked a paper through a hole in my curtain, then disappeared. I sat up. On the paper was written, in English, the words: 'I am taking the dust from your feet. Please come this side.' Again the head appeared. Blue Boy was urging me to come outside and engage in a ceremony with him. I knew what it would be: He would crouch at my feet, his head nearly on the ground, and either 'take dust from my feet' with his fingers and put it on his head, or actually (if he were really carried away) seize my foot and place it on his head.

"I got a pencil out of my shirt, and wrote by moonlight: 'Not necessary. Just go straight.' He glanced at the note and disappeared. I thought he had gone, but in fifteen minutes he was back with another note: evidently he had an accomplice—a schoolboy, judging from the handwriting—who knew English. This note said: 'I shall go straight. I shall obey you. I am coming your side.' I wrote back: 'I am going to sleep now. Good night.' Fifteen minutes later he was at my window again. Gazing steadfastly at me, he wrenched his head to one side—which must have meant something very emphatic—and disappeared.

"The next day I was returning to Bharat University by train, without Arjuna. By good luck I had obtained a tiny second-class compartment, and I was alone in it. I meant to sleep, for I had not slept a wink the night before. The train was passing over the great bridge which spans the Hooghly River—one of the mouths of the Ganges—and I was gazing peacefully down some hundreds of feet at the fishing boats gliding like toys over the brown water, when a set of dark brown fingers slid around the window frame on the outside, and clutched the bars. There was really nothing to walk on out there, and yet a man was pulling himself slowly along the outside of the car, and—there he was. It was Blue Boy, somberly staring in at me. I thought of pulling the emergency cord, but then I had a vision of a sudden lurching halt that would throw him off. I opened the door of the compartment. Very slowly and cautiously he crept along the space between the window and the door. Sinuous toes wriggled in at the door, then fingers, and then, all of a sudden, before I could leap back, Blue Boy was scrabbling at me on the dirty floor of the compartment. It is not easy to stand on one foot in a moving train. I fell heavily into the seat, tugging to get my foot free; but he had succeeded in getting it on top of his head. Apparently quite contented, Blue Boy remained seated on the floor, gazing up at me. For the first time, I saw him smile. He had won!

"In the confession which followed, Blue Boy, with alarming candor, told me that he was an untouchable from Orissa and that he had run away to Calcutta, posing as a 'dark' Brahman. And he did have a certain dignity about him that helped him carry it off. Blue Boy didn't *feel* inferior—that's what I liked about him. We agreed that, as far as that went, one fellow was about as touchable as the next. In fact, he said, he did not pick pockets in order to touch people, but merely to steal their money; for he had been unable to find work in Calcutta, and he hated to beg. Which would I prefer: begging or stealing?

"With a slight loan, which he is repaying, Blue Boy opened a tea shop in a town I shall not name. If the touch-me-not Brahmans of that town knew that the rather touchable young Brahman who serves them tea with such a touchingly elegant touch is the most lynchable untouchable imaginable—they would have 999 sacred touchy-fits."

It occurred to me then that the fellow in the blue Punjabi—the youthful tea-shop proprietor—who was leaning against the mango tree, watching my red-haired friend with such intensity, had not really degraded himself by groveling at Tino's feet. Nor had Tino, obviously. In a way, I thought, and allowing for exotic customs, it very likely fell into the same category and was as problematical as any other act of love.

The One Who Returns

Father Ryan had disappeared completely and mysteriously about two months before my arrival at the hill station of Rampoche on April 25, 1952. He had left the monastery in company with four other European priests and was hiking in the Himalayas somewhere near the frontier of Nepal. A botanist of sorts, he had strayed a few steps away from his party, with the intention of identifying a certain tree. His companions never saw him again, although they searched for him all the rest of that day. Sherpas, Lepchas, Tibetans, Nepalese, and several companies of Indian soldiers combed the whole area for a week, in vain.

It surprised me, rather, that a mysterious disappearance should make much of an impression on Rampoche. The town was surrounded by deep gorges and forests where I once saw a python lower ten feet of itself out of a tree to pull up a yelling thing that looked like a large sloth.

And there were the Yetis, the half-legendary, hairy man-like creatures who, I am now convinced, do really inhabit the upper slopes of the Himalayas. So far as I can recall, there is nothing funny about the Yeti except the English translation of the Tibetan word—which, if the truth be told, is not even Yeti—made by a charming man whose native tongue is not English. "The terrifying being who lives in the snows" thus becomes "the Abominable Snow Man"—a name that was quickly seized upon, not by true skeptics but by those who were determined not to believe; however, these were mere outsiders.

The people of the mountains know better. They evince a polite curiosity at the many photographs that have now been amassed, showing the huge footprints of the Yetis in the snow. These are common Yetis, though it is doubtful that the outsider will ever lay eyes on them, for they are masters of privacy. There are other Yetis who are far advanced in the ways of yoga.

And there is the Great Yeti, who is Illumined. His name must not be mentioned.

The story was told to me gradually, over a period of time, in several languages of men and of events; often imperceptibly: a word here or there, perhaps unnoticed at the time, dropped casually by some villager, shopkeeper, porter, or passing lama. For it was only the outsiders, like myself, who did not already know the truth.

One morning, not very early, but before the sun had hurdled the Himalayas, I was out splitting wood beside my cabin on the mountainside above Rampoche. A Tibetan lama in purple rags and a tall peaked cap came down the path. Standing before me and smiling, he began to jingle a little bell with one hand. With the other, he twirled a small drum on a handle, so that it was beaten by two dangling weights, one on each side. Then he sang. I remember the song perfectly, from that one hearing; but having tried once to sing it, I know that the song is his alone—perhaps because he possesses nothing in this world.

When he had sung, he blessed me until I felt blessed.

We squatted on the ground, not quite looking at each other, not quite not looking at each other, not able to concentrate on or to ignore the perpetual snows of Kinchinjunga, now suddenly kindled into flaming colors by the rising sun. My smile and his smile were the same. They did not belong to either of us. I experienced freedom and contentment, the invisible commodities of this wandering mendicant.

During a fit of madness brought on by dysentery, sentimentality, and the study of Sanskrit grammar, I had once insulted a Tibetan lama who came to me begging a bit too boisterously. I pushed him, I shouted curses at him, I threatened and nearly struck him with my brass opium pipe. And he laughed! Backing away in mock terror, the gigantic simpleton—the fool of God—thanked me for the experience. He walked away chortling, happier, if possible, than when he had first come.

Feelings of guilt now made me gauge my present lama's happiness by that of the former one. They seemed about the same, although I had given insults to the other one, and this Lama-ji was sharing my breakfast. Evidently I could have no effect upon either.

Lama-ji stirred butter into his tea and drank it with respect, crinkling his eyes at me.

"The Flat Land must be a very interesting place," he ventured politely.

I mentioned oceans, deserts, and peoples, and improvements in methods of transportation, communication, and government. However, he came straight to the point:

"Your Grand Lama is called a 'Pope,' is he not? Doubtless he is of a very high spiritual attainment?"

I told him that that was certainly the case, but that he had many troubles on account of the sin that is prevalent in the Flat Land.

Lama-ji murmured sympathetically.

"It is true," he said. "Father Ryan showed me a picture of the Pope Lama, and also one of the Illumined Jesus as a young man."

We changed the subject several times and then were silent. In this silence, all at once, I remembered that Father Ryan was the priest who had disappeared.

"Father Ryan," I said.

"We met on a hill before dawn," Lama-ji said, and I felt, looking at him, that he might be speaking metaphorically.

I continued to look at him.

"It was seven days before he was taken," he added.

I said: "I am ignorant. Please tell me what happened to him."

Lama-ji looked at me with surprise, then he said softly: "The Great Yeti took him—Yeti Guru."

I presumed that the Yeti had eaten Father Ryan.

Lama-ji laughed merrily.

"You are thinking of the big footprints in the snow," he said. "They are different. No, the Great Yeti is a spirit."

"Incarnated?"

"Yes, but he has no need to eat. Father Ryan is still alive."

"What is the Yeti like?"

"He is like a good and great yogi, but he is a boddhisattva, much bigger than men. He lives in a cave, high, very high up in the snows."

"Why has he taken Father Ryan?"

Lama-ji became very serious. With an awed expression he told me: "Sometimes the Great Yeti comes down from the snows to look at people. Usually he returns alone. But if he finds a human being with a pure soul, he will take that person with him. There in the cave Yeti Guru teaches the man, and the man receives Illumination."

"But the man does not return to the world?"

"At the end of six months he appears again among human beings in order to teach them. He has one month to do this, and at the end of that time—if he lives that long—he dies quickly and turns to dust. In that month he must stay in dark places, for he casts no shadow, and human beings are afraid at the approach of the Illumined One—and indeed he does make a great deal of trouble for them."

"What kind of trouble?" I asked.

"Ah," said Lama-ji sadly. "Men are provoked by the truth—as in your country they were provoked by the Illumined Jesus before he became a boddhisattva. Did they not burn him to ashes?"

"No," I said. "They crucified him."

"That is not fatal to One Who Returns," Lama-ji said. "Everyone knows that he must be burned to ashes, like a scroll. Otherwise he goes on teaching and disturbing people. You will see what happens when Father Ryan-Boddhisattva comes down from the snows."

Lama-ji's face was now serene, but with a suggestion of inward irony, a baffling combination of naïveté and sophistication.

"And whose side are you on?" I asked with some asperity.

Lama-ji quaked with suppressed laughter, some of which leaked out in little squeaks.

"My son," he said, "there are no sides. All is ritual."

At the end of June I went down to the Gangetic Plains. It was not until the following April that I returned to Rampoche to escape the heat. This time I made the acquaintance of Joan Venkataramanan, a handsome, learned, and courageous Englishwoman who had married an Indian. Daily she assaulted the Everest of her existence, and neither she nor it could ever admit defeat.

She and I and her two children were hiking along a mountain trail late one afternoon, when we stopped to sit on some boulders, to catch our breath. Joan was not a compulsive talker, but she talked steadily to me on that day for the simple reason that she had stored up so much that had to be told and could not be told —except to another inward sort of outsider. We sat there gazing out across immense depths and heights and distances of an indescribable grandeur. A black spot at the base of a mountain to our left loomed up curiously. I seemed to recall a white building. . . .

The children—a boy of seven and a girl of about ten—were

scampering up the mountainside in back of us. Joan was talking about freedom. It might be a good thing, she said, to be a nun for the sake of the *esprit de corps*—only, she was afraid of finding herself stuck without much *esprit* and no *corps* at all.

"I once knew an Irish priest who was a free spirit," Joan said. "He lived in a monastery that used to be down there, where you see that black spot—it burned down last October, with the abbot inside, and possibly someone else. The others were Belgians and a couple of Poles. Father Ryan—"

I suppose I looked intense, for Joan at once concentrated on this subject in order to remove any pretext I might have for interfering with her oblique confession. And indeed I did not wish to intrude. She was creating a world out of words. It was like the falling of snow. Under it lay Everest.

"The abbot," Joan was saying, "was a formidable man. I went to see him about the children's education, and we had a bit of a row. He was one of those granite-faced Walloons—a convert himself, I suspect. They always go to extremes to make up for their heretical past, you know."

Father Ryan, on the other hand, seemed to have been a good-hearted sort of fellow. He had given the children lessons in natural science until his superior, who may have feared Joan's possible influence on the teacher, forbade him to continue his friendship with them. Then Father Ryan had disappeared on that hiking expedition. . . .

And the monastery?

"Last October," Joan said, "the abbot did a terrible and heroic thing—I've been ashamed of myself ever since for having quarreled with him. Just after nightfall a fire broke out in the monastery. It must have been in the abbot's cell, because he was the only one who was aware of it.

"He rang the big bell—we heard it for miles around, wild and defiant—and he ordered everyone out of the monastery. Then he locked the gates to keep anyone from coming back in. He stayed in there alone to fight the fire, and he died in there. It was foolish of him—with help he might have put out the fire—but he wouldn't risk the lives of the others. I can hardly understand such absolute courage, can you? Within an hour the place was in ashes.

"Of course, you know how people like to embroider simple events. Some of the monks claimed to have seen a shadowy figure at nightfall moving majestically out of the forest, into the monastery, and up to the abbot's room, which was in a sort of tower. That was just before the fire started.

"Then there was that unstable Polish monk, a sort of menial. When the flames were at their height, he saw in them a vision of Christ—smiling ever so slightly, seated in the padmasana, or lotus posture, His hands raised in the mudra of Divine Teaching."

The children were coming down the mountain toward us. I began to convey to Joan, by gestures, a certain restlessness that had taken hold of me. It was getting late, and after nightfall the trails in those precipitous mountains are not altogether safe, especially for the outsider whose gaze may be momentarily distracted by the sight of moonlight on snow over a considerable area and at some height.

◀◖◖◖◖◖◖◖◖◖◀▷ *The Lover of Bharatpur*

Under the full moon a man was baying. As he circled the mud hut, he paused at the barred and shuttered windows. On the door fell the shadow of his upraised arms holding a club. Then it was ominously quiet. For a moment the club was raised high against the flimsy wooden door; and the man within, watching through a crack, stood back clutching a piece of iron. The madman dropped the club and ran away without striking. As he ran he sobbed mysterious words of compassion that echoed through the still, heavy night of the Bengal plain:

"Poor God! Poor, *poor* God!"

Cautiously, after some minutes had passed, Aretino Scott opened the shutters and looked out through the wooden bars, but he left the door closed and bolted. It would take a bit of doing, he thought, for Jimmy Powers to come through the thatched roof. Still, this was no night to sleep. He sat on the edge of the low wooden platform that served as a bed, and prepared to keep watch.

Someone obviously had told Jimmy about the council of foreigners who had met to consider him as a problem. And it was one of the council who had done it, perhaps to turn him against Aretino and the other Americans at Bharat University. Jimmy felt betrayed by his friends. But who had betrayed the betrayers? Who was the archtraitor among them? For the council had meant to be discreet. They were not monsters. They had merely met, spontaneously and in self-defense, to decide what on earth to do about Jimmy, and they had come to no definite conclusion. Some fool or mischief-maker among them had set him off by informing him—judging from his ravings—that everyone was plotting against him.

Jimmy's papers had been in good order, and he had been accepted as a special student at Bharat University, where he would study Indian art. During his tempestuous three weeks there, he had created consternation, not only among the Indians but still more among the foreigners. He was mad, of that there was no doubt; for he offered love in all directions, without giving a thought as to race, creed, color, caste, age, or condition, and he did not know that he was guilty. It was unnerving to consider the probable extent of Jimmy's conquests, if they could be called that. They were not really conquests, but kindnesses; for he gave himself as he gave all his other possessions, unreservedly and for the sake of love. The fact that he was simple, guileless, and to the point, was one-third of the victory; that his face was fair and child-like, with a bloom of physical health and youth, and his body well formed, was another third—though not necessarily definitive; but in addition to these things, he was so vulnerable that none could strike. Therein lay his magic. Only the most pitiless of love objects could resist him entirely.

When the beggars came to this little university town, as they did every Friday, mewing and gibbering and showing their treasured defects, they concentrated on the new foreigner. For foreigners are not only ignorant of custom, they are also easily upset, unpredictable, and munificent. The vulture-like throng surrounded Jimmy, moaning and lurching against him. Jimmy took one look at them, sat down on the ground, and cried, moaning in sympathy with them. Then he stood up, his face working spasmodically, tears coursing down his cheeks, and began handing out money; then he wrote checks. As their greed made them clamor all the more, he gave them his wrist watch, his ring, his wallet. They showed him their rags, crying piteously. Jimmy stripped himself and gave them his shoes and his clothes, every stitch, and stood there stark naked, patting their ugly heads, stroking their diseased faces, embracing their corpse-like bodies. The beggars backed away and became silent; they looked at one another; they looked at Jimmy, and they were abashed. They tried to give him back some of his clothes, but Jimmy shook his head and wiped his eyes. "No, no!" he sobbed. "*You* take them! Poor, poor God! Oh, *poor* God!" And all of Bharatpur was treated to the spectacle of the naked and lamenting American walking down the road surrounded by a pack of beggars who were trying to persuade him to take his clothes back.

The person who had been most impressed by the spiritual possibilities of this scene was lovely, witty, dark-haired Mlle. de Rosière, the French Buddhist. Aretino Scott, the American, was in love with her. So were Mr. Kashani, the bearded little Persian, and Dr. Wilhelm Fraunhofer, the German authority on the Sanskrit aorist, whom she despised. The general opinion was that Aretino had been gradually outmaneuvering the Buddha for her affections—until the incident of the beggars.

There were other observers of that incident. Dr. Fraunhofer's brother Karl and Karl's wife Katy—both American citizens— had taken a house nearby, for a month or two. Dr. Karl Fraunhofer was the American authority on the Structure of the Buddhist Hell in Prakrit Texts, and he was thriftily combining a visit with his brother with some research on his specialty. Katy Fraunhofer, of Russian origin, was exceedingly American; that is, she was red-blooded and warmhearted, unlike other nationalities. Seeing Jimmy, an American, mother-naked, as it were, and pursued by heathen devils, she seized him by the hand and drew him into that island of safety, her house. It was saturated with DDT and Lysol. Imported screens on windows and doors kept out the proliferating life of India. Within a few minutes Jimmy's tears were dried and he was dressed in Professor Karl Fraunhofer's best seersucker suit. Then she produced doughnuts. Katy Fraunhofer became Jimmy's mother, as it were.

There was a curious competition among the foreigners—especially the women—to endure Jimmy; and the occasion arose for each of them several times a day. They could not conceal themselves from him, for he would call out, laughing, "I know you're in there!" in such cozening tones that they must either come out or let him in. But to be with him was to be embarrassed, if not—in some cases—compromised; for in the moment of surprised or kindly indecision, impulse sometimes had its way. Forbearance was merely the first step toward the fall; but falling was not always painful, if there were no witnesses. And Jimmy was no witness. He had no more sense of sin than a butterfly. Besides, he could not stay long—it was written.

Janina, the mysterious young Polish woman, was one of the witnesses of the beggar scene, who learned to endure him. She had endured the Nazi occupation of her country; from the Russian occupation she had escaped, it was said, by walking. The story went that she had walked safely through Afghanistan. In India she lived by her wits, obtaining a number of university scholarships from the Indian Government, at the same time warding off deportation by a series of long, complicated letters to the Ministry of External Affairs, who always took at least six months to reply. Meanwhile, her decorum was above reproach—until the arrival of Jimmy. Her rigid discipline, of years' standing, was shattered by the desire to be something like a big sister to him. And her only frustration lay in the amazing number of big and little sisters with whom she must share him.

Olga Basu, the disoriented Russian widow of an Indian, was perhaps Jimmy's principal beneficiary. For thirty of her fifty-three years she had been married to a famous swami, twenty years older than she. Though sophisticated in things of the spirit, he was appallingly ignorant in other matters. Having failed once or twice to consummate the marriage, he had withdrawn perma-

nently to the "higher life" and had prevailed on Olga to do like-
wise. The criminal had died two years ago, leaving his virgin
widow rather unprepared to meet the world. In desperation—for
she was a vigorous woman beneath the collapsing superstructure
of her spirituality—she had looked about her. Indeed, being now
somewhat deranged, she had made a nuisance of herself with
handsome young men such as Aretino Scott. Then Jimmy Powers
had come, and he had not rejected her at all. Miraculously he had
transcended her age and her fat; her madness effaced itself in
homage to his.

Dr. Jonathan Leapsheets, the exchange professor from Canada,
appreciated the therapeutic effects of Jimmy's love in the case
of Olga. Before becoming a sociologist, Leapsheets had been a
consulting psychologist. Nothing much surprised him any more.
If Diana, his handsome, sullen wife, who had been one of his
patients in the old days, chose now to submit the psychotic
American to some form of occupational therapy, he could hardly
do less than advise her with his greater knowledge and experience.
Although they had, in truth, little hope for Jimmy's ultimate ad-
justment and integration, nevertheless they took a strong personal
interest in his case.

The periphery of Jimmy's acquaintance extended beyond Dr.
Wu Lu's mother—an awful old crone, heavy with ornaments—
into a shadowy, apparently limitless field among the Indian population. Everyone in Bharatpur knew what was happening, for
it was an ingrown little community, already full of conflicts, and
any intensification of intrigue was immediately felt by all. In the
eyes of the Indians, the foreigners had become involved in an
extraordinary scandal, to which, of course, foreigners are prone
—reason enough for politely leaving them to their own devices.
But the Indians themselves were involved. There is something
about a conspicuous madman: a challenge, perhaps, to surpass
other men in saintly forbearance, patience, fortitude, wisdom,
transcendental love, and so forth; these were among the virtues

they lavished on Jimmy, but these were only beginnings. Not only the officials, but the faculty members, began to question their wives and to be dissatisfied with the answers; the students were demoralized, as well as the genteel families who basked in the aura of culture about the university, and had nothing to do and plenty of opportunities; and the villagers: Brahmans, Kshatriyas, Vaisyas, Sudras; and the untouchables. The Santals, happy black aborigines, loved him without knowing that he was mad: if he went naked and made love, nothing could be more natural.

Jimmy was not jealous. Like Brahma, he was wholly present, fulfilled, and debonair in each particular relationship. But his lovers were not so disinterested. They tolerated or invited or pursued him for what they could get out of him, not least of which was the flattery of his complete attention at the time. They knew, perhaps, that the god was blind, but they could not afford to believe that he was blind in their particular case. Theirs was a personal relation to an impersonal god. And everybody suffered an upset schedule.

Jimmy was never still for long. He moved like a bright stream of water, flowing around obstacles, into innumerable nooks and crannies, offering itself inexhaustibly, taking everything by surprise. It was a festive time, a time of jangled nerves, of confusion and recrimination. Sometimes people confronted him angrily, but their reasons were beyond his comprehension. If they would not accept him—which meant permitting his embraces—then his spirit became clouded. His head drooping to one side, as in the Pietà of Michelangelo, or like a Rouault clown, "Poor God!" he would murmur brokenly, with infinite compassion. "Poor, poor God!" No one knew quite what this meant, and he could not tell them. Nor did he mean it to be effective. It was unnerving. "Kindly explain the American cultural-metaphysical depth implications of this ejaculation!" Dr. Wilhelm Fraunhofer once demanded of Aretino Scott, who had to confess that he also was mystified. And Mlle. de Rosière, in a little French conversation with Aretino, ventured the theory that Jimmy's reference was to a god who was *limited,* or perhaps chained like Prometheus.

"Human beings are irresistibly attracted by chains," she said, "by the blind charm of the somnambule, by the helplessness of the slavey, by the soldier in the anonymous uniform. These are not free, but chained like victims. They do not present us with the resistance of individuality; they are helpless, no? We feed on them—"

"Or they on us?"

"It is the same thing, *mon cher* Aretino. We abandon them; there are no consequences, no responsibilities."

"They are not responsible either," Aretino said. "That is the danger, and it is mutual."

"You are troubled? It is all Maya, a game of illusion."

"Am I such a repulsive person?" he asked. "Is there some element in me of which I am unaware, to which you cannot in the nature of things respond?"

"But no." She laughed. "You are splendid: the hair red-gold, the eyes Italianate, the skin pure ivory. These things naturally appeal to me."

"But perhaps a languor, also from my Italian mother?"

"No, no, you are not without fanaticism; but you are not—not mad, like Jimmy! You do not so much need the Teaching of the Buddha—or rather, you do not admit it so much by your actions. You are neither foolish nor desperate, my dear. But you are such a good friend, how shall I say it to you—"

"I am not your friend," Aretino said angrily. "I love you, such as I am, and that—that animal can't love anyone—"

"He loves in a way that you do not understand," said Marie de Rosière. "He loves as God loves, with a slight difference. And now, M. Aretino, I am fatigued—"

In Bengal it is good manners to embrace and kiss one's friends and to walk about hand in hand with them—provided that they are not women. One must not touch a woman, unless she happens to be one's sister. Jimmy could not help touching and embracing the girls also, as if he regarded them all as sisters. One day he picked up and cradled in his arms a sour-faced Bengali girl, who promptly had a fit of hysterics. That was the last straw. A citizens' committee called on the vice chancellor of the university, and the V.C., not knowing quite what to do—international politics being possibly at stake, he thought—had an interview with Jimmy; and Jimmy promised to try to do better, but he laid his head in the V.C.'s lap and wept, then smiled up at him, and the V.C. was considerably rattled. One simply did not know where to draw the line between idiosyncrasies and national characteristics. Perhaps it was the reserved Aretino Scott, with the odd name, who was the atypical one, and this Jimmy Powers was the representative American!

It might have gone on for some time longer had it not been for the dinner at the V.C.'s house. The only Indians present were the V.C. and the registrar and their wives, whose unenviable karma required that they entertain the foreign scholars once a year. It was a grim business, that dinner. Chairs that martyred the flesh were squared off against one another in geometrical opposition, and they were not to be moved. People sat facing each other stiffly, at precise distances. The V.C. and the registrar sat like policemen at opposite ends of the table. At the V.C.'s right were Dr. Wilhelm Fraunhofer, the registrar's wife, U Aung (the Burmese scholar), Mlle. de Rosière, Aretino Scott, Katy Fraunhofer, Mr. Kashani, and the V.C.'s wife. To the left of the V.C. were Olga Basu, Jimmy Powers, Janina, Dr. Wu Lu, Diana Leapsheets, Dr. Karl Fraunhofer, Mme. Wu, and Dr. Jonathan Leapsheets. It was the entire foreign contingent of the university, and this dinner was expected to appease for one year their persistent but vain hunger for a social life.

The presence of so many people in one room generated in Jimmy a vast happiness. He talked and gestured and laughed with abnormal vivacity; his face was roseate and glorious; and his words sparkled and tumbled forth like fireworks, crazy and witty and naïvely, tenderly, lovingly pornographic. Fortunately he spoke rapid, colloquial American, which was mostly unintelligible to all of his captive audience except Aretino Scott, and perhaps Katy Fraunhofer. It was impossible to escape from Jimmy's orbit even for a moment. Like the sun, he could only release his greater vitality and be the self-consuming source and center of things.

All at once he sank back in his chair like a saint in ecstasy, his face melting with joy. On his right Olga shrieked, then began to giggle and blush. To his left, Janina sat up straight and severe and pale, her long upper lip drawn down over her teeth as her sari was drawn down over her knees. Suddenly she leaped up, then sat down again, two spots of red appearing on her cheeks. Turning her big gray eyes on Jimmy, she delivered a reproachful look. Jimmy's head drooped, tears welled up in his eyes. Taking her hand, he kissed it, then laid it on his head, but this time he did not say "Poor God!" Janina glanced about, as if wondering how much people knew; then she smiled tremulously.

Before the evening was over, Jimmy had taken liberties with nearly everyone, and for one reason or another, nobody could gather himself or herself sufficiently to be really cruel to him, and he could not grasp ordinary, civilized rebuffs. He had the initiative; it would be necessary to reach a point of intensity greater than that of his enamored fury, in order to overcome him. Perhaps some of the guests were not without force of character, but there were complications of one sort or another: pity for a young madman, respect for the Fool of God who lives truths that ordinary people find it inconvenient to speak, aesthetic appreciation and, closely related to this, a whole range of secret responses, some perhaps deeply hidden in the unconscious. And there was the desire for the victory of the irrational over a foolishly rational scheme of things that satisfied nobody. Jimmy was the nihilist, the illegal protagonist of all. At least the dinner was not the funeral the V.C. had intended!

At the earliest possible moment, while Jimmy was embracing the V.C. and kissing the feet of his wife—and they did not defend themselves very well, partly because they were not absolutely certain that it was not an American custom—Aretino Scott slunk out. Hardly had he reached his hut, when Dr. and Mrs. Leapsheets and Mlle. de Rosière arrived, followed by Katy and Karl and Wilhelm Fraunhofer, Mr. Kashani and Janina, then by Dr. Wu Lu and Mme. Wu and U Aung. Silently they crowded in and sat on wicker stools and the bed, avoiding one another's eyes. They huddled there in silence for a long moment, then several started talking at once.

"If you can't love him," Dr. Leapsheets was saying, "anyway don't persecute him. He will go away soon. He must."

"Who persecutes him?" Janina turned her big gray eyes on the Canadian. "If I push him off, I persecute him? No, no, he is a love-maker. It is he who persecutes. We should tell the American consul in Calcutta."

"And what would you say?" It was Mlle. de Rosière. "Would you say, He makes love at me, take him away? The consul would say, But he is *galant* and it is comprehensible, or similar things, no?"

"No, no," Janina said. "We have our work to do, and he has disturbed our schedule. Therefore, he must be—controlled."

"Pardon me," Mr. Kashani said, and his eyes were very eloquent, as they always were. "I believe in the *noblesse* of the human, like Tagore. If one approaches to him with *sincérité* and *autorité*, he will respond. If you request to me, I will say him: You are good boy, you have *pureté* of heart, but you do not consider. He will say: What I should do? I will say: Consider before you make love. Perhaps it is not *propre!*"

"I am responsible," Aretino Scott began. "You are responsible. We—"

"Not all of us," said Mme. Wu maliciously. "Not all are here." It was understood that she meant Olga, who should now be quite happy. At last she had found a lover, even if he was a lunatic!

"All, *ja*, all," cried Dr. Wilhelm Fraunhofer, "all stand within the same circle of corruptibility, and all are obligated by the same Categorical Imperative." He glanced at his Russian-American sister-in-law, and his face became more strained looking than ever—Katy was staring at him, with the insolent rudeness that is made possible by the consciousness of power. "We should be kind to the person discussed," he concluded hastily, "and learn from him to love one another. Can you not understand this?" Again, a glance at Katy.

Coming from Fraunhofer, it sounded like a bad joke. The council of foreigners—all except Katy and Karl—stared in dismay at the authority on the Sanskrit aorist. Because of his habit of making harsh moral judgments, they had taken it for granted that he would be firmly hostile to Jimmy, that it would, indeed, be necessary to moderate his savagery in order to achieve a humane solution, and that he would, if all else failed, be their spokesman to the officials of the university. In short, they had so far counted on his extremism to carry the point, that they themselves had not troubled to take a really strong position. And now, not only could he not be counted on, he had undermined them, shamed them, beat them all at the game of charity.

"It is more blessed to give than to receive," Katy Fraunhofer said in a ringing voice.

"Maybe yes, maybe no," Diana replied, rising to go, "but it is more problematical to receive."

Nothing more came of the meeting, except a vague annoyance with Americans and an increased respect and detestation for Wilhelm Fraunhofer; for he had indeed practiced what he preached. The progress of the Definitive Treatise on the Sanskrit Aorist was at a standstill.

"That," said Jonathan Leapsheets petulantly, as Wilhelm took leave of them, "is a true Christian?"

Katy Fraunhofer remained after the others had gone—Karl lingered uncertainly in the shadows. "Listen to me, Scotty," Katy said, standing in the middle of the room. "I've got something to say, and I'm gonna say it right now."

"Shoot," said Aretino.

Katy weighed that word; weighed also Aretino; coolly lighted a cigarette before continuing: "What I've got to say is this: We Americans ought to stick together, see? These foreigners and natives, you can't trust 'em. They're all a lot of communists. If I had my way, I'd see that quite a few of 'em were liquidated."

Aretino turned pale with rage, and his voice trembled: "Mrs. Fraunhofer, I am in absolute and total disagreement with you on every possible subject."

Katy disregarded this. "What I want to know is, How come they all swarmed into this hut of yours? How come they didn't call on me and Karl?" The naïveté of her question was in such contrast to the craftiness of her expression that Aretino decided she must be mad also. His face relaxed in a crooked, ancient smile. He shrugged his most Italian shrug.

Some time during the night, after Jimmy's siege of the hut, Aretino dozed off. At dawn he was awakened by a noise outside his window. Grasping the piece of iron in his right hand, he cautiously opened the shutter with his left. It was Mlle. de Rosière. For a brief moment she stood in his embrace.

"I heard him weeping," she said. "It was terrible. I did not dare to let him in. He ran down Gualpara Road in the night. I found a rickshaw and followed him—to the railway station."

"Marie, he is violent! Why did you do it—or do you really love him?"

"I love him," she said slowly, "but in a manner that is not exclusive. Perhaps you will understand someday."

"I will try," Aretino said.

"Perhaps you will become a little like him. Already, perhaps—Aretino, my friend, I have come to ask you to go after him, to see that no harm befalls him. He jumped on the train that goes to Calcutta, and he is without shoes or coat or hat. I think he has no money. There are those in Calcutta who have no comprehension, and there are those who are wicked."

"I will go," said Aretino.

The next train to Calcutta would not leave until the afternoon. Just as Aretino was starting for the station, the vice chancellor sent for him. The Calcutta police had telephoned. Jimmy had been arrested for disturbing the peace, and had been paroled to the American consul at the suggestion of Professor Karl Fraunhofer. Would Aretino, as Jimmy's friend and fellow countryman, be responsible for collecting his effects and sending them to him? It seemed quite likely that he would not return.

After some weeks a letter arrived for Aretino from the States. It was written in a large, childish hand. From a state hospital for the insane Jimmy sent his respects to all his friends at Bharatpur:

". . . Mr. Kashani was right, I did not consider. Please forgive Katy for telling me about your plot. Love is greater than anyone. I have so much to learn! Now I am going deeply into myself. I was here before, you know. I was not ready to come into the world. . . ."

"Poor God!" Aretino muttered.

THREE TALES

◥◤◥◤◥◤◥◤ *The Listener**

Once there was a puny little Czech concert violinist named Rudolf, who lived in Sweden. Some of his friends thought he was not the best of musicians because he was restless; others thought he was restless because he was not the best of musicians. At any rate, he hit upon a way of making a living, with no competitors. Whether by choice or necessity, he used to sail about Scandinavia in his small boat, all alone, giving concerts in little seaport towns. If he found accompanists, well and good; if not, he played works for unaccompanied violin; and it happened once or twice that he wanted a piano so badly that he imagined one, and then he played whole sonatas for violin and piano, with no piano in sight.

One year Rudolf sailed all the way out to Iceland and began working his way around that rocky coast from one town to another. It was a hard, stubborn land; but people in those difficult places do not forget the law of hospitality to the stranger—for their God may decree that they too shall become strangers on the face of the earth. The audiences were small, and even if Rudolf had been really first-rate they would not have been very demonstrative. From ancient times their energy had gone, first of all, into earnest toil. Sometimes they were collected by the local schoolteacher, who reminded them of their duty to the names

* Karl Almegaard told me this story. If it were not true, he would not have told it.

103

of Beethoven and Bach and Mozart and one or two others whose music perhaps was not much heard in those parts. Too often people sat stolidly watching the noisy little fiddler, and went home feeling gravely edified. But they paid.

As Rudolf was sailing from one town to the next along a sparsely settled shore, the northeast turned black and menacing. A storm was bearing down upon Iceland. Rudolf was rounding a bleak, dangerous cape, and his map told him that the nearest harbor was half a day's journey away. He was beginning to worry, when he saw, less than a mile offshore, a lighthouse on a tiny rock island. At the base of the lighthouse was a deep, narrow cove, protected by cliffs. With some difficulty in the rising seas, he put in there and moored to iron rings that hung from the cliff. A flight of stairs, hewn out of the rock, led up to the lighthouse. On top of the cliff, outlined against the scudding clouds, stood a man.

"You are welcome!" the voice boomed over the sound of the waves that were already beginning to break over the island.

Darkness fell quickly. The lighthouse keeper led his guest up the spiral stairs to the living room on the third floor, then busied himself in preparation for the storm. Above all, he had to attend to the great lamp in the tower, that dominated the whole region. It was a continuous light, intensified by reflectors, and eclipsed by shutters at regular intervals. The duration of light was equal to that of darkness.

The lighthouse keeper was a huge old man with a grizzled beard that came down over his chest. Slow, deliberate, bear-like, he moved without wasted motion about the limited world of which he was the master. He spoke little, as if words had not much importance compared to the other forces that comprised his life. Yet he was equable, as those elements were not.

After the supper of black bread and boiled potatoes, herring, cheese, and hot tea, which they took in the kitchen above the living room, the two men sat and contemplated each other's presence. Above them was the maintenance room, and above that the great lamp spoke majestic, silent messages of light to the ships at sea. The storm hammered like a battering ram on the walls of the lighthouse. Rudolf offered tobacco, feeling suddenly immature as he did so. The old man smiled a little as he declined it by a slight movement of the head; it was as if he knew well the uses of tobacco and the need for offering it, and affirmed it all, yet—here he, too, was halfway apologetic—was self-contained and without need of anything that was not already within his power or to which he did not relinquish his power. And he sat there, gentle and reflective, his great workman hands resting on outspread thighs.

It seemed to Rudolf that the lighthouse keeper was entirely aware of all the sounds of the storm and of its violent impact upon the lighthouse but that he knew them so well he did not have to think about them; they were like the involuntary movements of his own heart and blood. In the same way, beneath the simple courtesy that made him speak and listen to his guest in specific ways, he was already calmly and mysteriously a part of him, as surely as the mainland was connected with the little island, and all the islands with each other, so commodiously under the ocean.

Gradually Rudolf drew forth the sparse data of the old man's life: he had been born in this very lighthouse eighty-three years before, when his father was the lighthouse keeper. His mother— the only woman he had ever known—had taught him to read the Bible, and he read it daily. He had no other books.

As a musician, Rudolf had not had time to read much either— but then, he had lived in cities. He reached down and took his beloved violin out of its case.

"What do you make with that, sir?" the old man asked.

For a second Rudolf thought his host might be joking; but the serenity of the other's expression reassured him. There was not even curiosity about the instrument, but rather a whole interest in him, the person, that included his "work." In most circumstances Rudolf would have found it hard to believe that there could exist someone who did not know what a violin was; yet now he had no inclination to laugh. He felt small and inadequate.

"I make—music with it," he stammered in a low voice.

"Music," the old man said ponderously. "I have heard of it. But I have never seen music."

"One does not see music. One hears it."

"Ah, yes," the lighthouse keeper consented, as it were with humility. This too was in the Nature of Things wherein all works were wonders, and all things were known eternally and were poignant in their transiency. His wide gray eyes rested upon the little fiddler and conferred upon him all the importance of which any individual is capable.

Then something in the storm and the lighthouse and the old man exalted Rudolf, filled him with compassion and love and a spaciousness infinitely beyond himself. He wanted to strike a work of fire and stars into being for the old man. With the storm as his accompanist, he stood and began to play the Kreutzer Sonata of Beethoven.

The moments passed, moments that were days in the creation of that world of fire and stars: abysses and heights of passionate struggle, the Idea of Order, and the resolution of these in the greatness of the human spirit. Never before had Rudolf played with such mastery—or with such an accompanist. Waves and wind beat the tower with giant hands. Steadily above them the beacon blazed in its sure cycles of darkness and light. The last note ceased, and Rudolf dropped his head on his chest, breathing hard. The ocean seethed over the island with a roar as of many voices.

The old man had sat unmoving through the work, his broad, gnarled hands resting on his thighs, his head bowed, listening massively. For some time he continued to sit in silence. Then he looked up, lifted those hands calmly, judiciously, and nodded his head.

"Yes," he said. "That is true."

∗∢∢∢∢∢∢∢∢∢∢∢   *The Sibling*

Marguerite didn't mind in the least being what she was, perhaps because she was indifferent to boys. She did her work cheerfully and humbly, sewing for a living, in a little house on the edge of town. The boys were not indifferent to her, though. They pestered her and hooted and whistled when she walked down the street; they drew symbols on her door; they threw rocks at her house. Their reason for persecuting her was very simple: She had a remarkably sweet and pretty face which attracted them too far in view of the fact that she had a big hump on her back. Anyone who loved such a person would have some tall explaining to do. Parents would say: "A pretty face is not enough, but a hump is too much." So the boys hated her, rather as if she had been a gentle, pretty boy. The girls hated her because she was an orphan (some people have all the luck) and because she did not do what they would have done if they had been orphans. The adults despised her because she never asked for charity, never seemed to need anything they had—was not even lonely! "How can such a creature be unlonely!" they snorted. "Even *we* are lonely! Who does she think she is, a society unto herself?"

The priest disliked her because he suspected her of withholding important information from him during confession; nevertheless it was his duty to give her spiritual guidance. "Living in a nightmare world is not as bad as people think," he said kindly. "Being a world, it contains good and evil; where the good is relative, naturally the evil is relative too." Marguerite knew how to get along in her world. She was astute; she was well adjusted; she knew how to find the areas of lesser discomfort, to play one horror off against another.

All was as it should be, until the beautiful stranger came to town. He had a mass of kinky golden hair, and the enormous dark, self-absorbed eyes of a baby giraffe; tall and shapely he was, and he wore carnival clothes of a sort that would have landed him in jail immediately had not the police hit on the idea of keeping him under surveillance in order to catch him at something still worse. His name was Paris. The women hated him. The men hated him. Everybody hated him—except Marguerite. From the morning she caught him gazing at the symbols the boys had chalked on her door during the night, she loved him. The rapture on his face had filled her with rapture.

What is one to do under such circumstances? One goes to the doctor. Marguerite had never been to the doctor, although several people had urged her to do so—even the priest, his mortal enemy. The priest hated him for disseminating free information about birth control, drinking, atheism, and the like, for giving advice and for being otherwise charitable outside the Church.

"If that despicable man rids you of your hump so that you can live contrary to God's wishes," said the priest, "he will pay for it in the hereafter. If he tries and fails, he will be ruined in this world as well, even if he escapes hanging. Finally, as a result of all this, it seems quite possible to me that you may have a baby. I can see that man's chagrin! I cannot help thinking that the moral which I shall point out afterward will outweigh the actual harm done. Go ahead, Marguerite, consult him."

Thick, heavy snow lay over the countryside, over the town, beautifying everything except the grotesque hump of a girl in love. Pulling her unusually long, warm shawl about her shoulders, she trudged down the street to the ramshackle house where the doctor had his office. The man of science sat behind his desk, drawing venomous little faces on his fingernails with a fountain pen. After a moment he glanced at Marguerite, put the pen down, grabbed a sheaf of papers, and muttered, "I'm a busy man."

"I realize that," Marguerite faltered, "and I wouldn't have bothered you—if it weren't for—"

"Well, what is it—some sort of disgusting female thing, or do you have a cough?"

"Neither, sir. It's—"

"Nerves, or I miss my guess." The doctor stood up, chuckled, started to pat her on the back, then thought better of it.

"It's this hump," she mumbled, tugging ineffectually at both ends of her shawl.

The doctor wagged his head, sighed, and sat down.

"You are dissatisfied with it?"

"Oh, no, sir, not dissatisfied exactly—but I was wondering— would it be possible—could you make it, perhaps, just a trifle less conspicuous?"

"I suppose the priest put you up to this," he said, and for a moment he looked as if he were going to cry. "I am not unfamiliar with his methods. He knows that such an operation is impossible under the primitive conditions I have to work with in this God-forsaken town. If I send you to Copenhagen, he can say that I am trying to get you out of the way, to disembarrass myself. If I take you there myself, he will say that I am seducing you, or that in spite of all my medical knowledge, I have already planted a fetus somewhere in your genitourinary mechanism. If, on the other hand, I should perform the impossible—"

"You will!" Marguerite said with a kind of irrational joy that upset the poor doctor still further.

"—then he will hold me responsible for the immoral life you will undoubtedly lead in order to make up for the time you have lost because of this hump, to which you owe your chastity."

"I swear to you—"

"Swear me no oaths," he said wearily. "Do you want to perjure yourself before an atheist? If I fail, you will die. . . . Why are you smiling? The operation is illegal in this province. I shall be hanged and publicly castigated, and I shall probably deserve it."

"The priest did say something of the sort," she murmured, "but he takes a great deal for granted. I think that you are right and he is wrong. There is no God."

The doctor stared at her pensively for a long moment; then he took a pencil from his coat pocket and began cleaning his nails with the sharp lead point. They got blacker and blacker. The little faces he had drawn on them glared around with renewed intensity.

"Tell me," he said, "is there some particular man whom you wish to attract, or will any man do? There are men in the world who have precisely your type of affliction, and although their problem is not often conducive to dispositions as sweet as yours —ah, then!" Marguerite was in tears. "So it is some particular man! What is his name?"

"Paris," said Marguerite.

"Ugh! That one! It is for him that you wish to undergo this unusually revolting operation?"

"For him I would do anything—anything! Life would not be worth living without him. He has looked at me with compassion."

"I understand perfectly," the doctor said, "and although I am not a religious man, I find myself barely able to forgive you for such a blunder. Paris is no good."

"But he *is* good! He *is*! He is Truth, Beauty, and Goodness!"

"You poor child, Paris is hopelessly autoerotic."

"Then I will help him—I know I can!"

"No, you can't. He doesn't want you, doesn't need you, doesn't need anybody."

"Perhaps you're a little jealous of his independence, Doctor?" she asked cunningly.

"Jealous of Narcissus?"

"Ah, Narcissus," she sighed. "He loved the pool for the beauty he saw reflected in it, and the pool loved him for the beauty it saw reflected in his eyes. The beauty of the pool and the beauty of Narcissus—they were the same. They were never separated, those two. When he died—"

"Never mind finishing the myth," the doctor said irritably. "I see you have learned a thing or two from the priest. Already you have separated Narcissus from his pool. Words, words! Take your clothes off."

"Take—my—"

"Yes, damn it! Hurry up! Rip off those rags and throw your ugly carcass on that table, so that I can see the extent of the curse which your hairy fiend Jehovah has inflicted on you!"

"Oh, no! I can't, I never can! Never, never!"

"Why not, idiot?"

"I should never have come here, I know that now. But I tried —I made a beautiful high collar, a sort of ruff, and a sort of bustle to wear down below, you see, to take up the slack in the dress so that it wouldn't be so noticeable—and my hair flowing down over everything—but it wouldn't work, it just wouldn't!" Marguerite was in hysterics, wringing her hands and weeping.

"Drink this," the doctor said, handing her a glass of water into which he had dropped a white powder. "It will help you to compose yourself. Now then, tell me a little more about this complaint of yours."

"Oh, sir, it isn't a complaint, it's a joy—that's what makes it so difficult."

"I see. Well, well. This problem, then. This hump or hunch or whatever you call it. When did you first notice it?"

"Not until people called my attention to it."

"And when was that?"

"It must have been when I was about eleven or twelve years old."

"I see. And what did your mother say?"

"She said it was my cross."

"Anything else?"

"Doctor," said Marguerite with dignity, laying her hand upon his pencil to prevent him from resuming his nail cleaning, "I know you mean well, but there are certain things which I am bound never to reveal, and this is one of them. Let us get on with the cure, I beg of you."

"I realize," the doctor said, playing for time, "that families have their secrets, some of which are transmitted through the genes. However, every horror becomes fashionable sooner or later, somewhere in the world. For example, circumcision was secretly practiced in my family for at least three centuries because of a peculiar drapery with which the male children are born. It started, I believe, under the Ottoman Empire, when the heirs of my family were forced, because of these very draperies, to serve as decorations in the entourages of jaded pashas."

"My situation is not like that," Marguerite said—the drug was beginning to work, so that she sounded less sure of herself. "My mother said that I must never tell, that no one must ever see. She bound me by a terrible oath. Now do you understand?"

"Perfectly," said the doctor.

"But"—Marguerite looked down at her hands and squirmed under her burden, and in that uncertain light the hump seemed enormous, glowering, baleful—"she did not say that no one must ever feel it."

The doctor closed his eyes and shuddered at the thought of laying his hands on the malformation in pitch darkness. After a moment, fortified by a long drink from a bottle he kept hidden in his desk for just such emergencies, he opened the door to a large closet. "In there."

Pale and resolute, the girl went into the closet with the doctor. In that confined space the sound of their breathing was terribly loud. It seemed to have an echo. Marguerite began to weep.

"Imagine that I am your mother," the doctor said gently, caressing her and running his hands over her. The coarse woolen dress came off over her head, the cotton chemise dropped to her feet. Marguerite stood naked and trembling while the doctor explored. In a way he was glad of the darkness now. If she could see his grimaces, she would hardly feel reassured! "I see," he croaked at length, rubbing his damp, icy hands on the seat of his trousers. "Well, well. A not uncommon condition after all. The only difference is in the manner of juncture. Generally siblings of your sort are joined either face to face or back to back. However, the ventral surface of the atrophied partner, in this instance, appears to be attached to the dorsal surface of the stronger, more perfect organism—if one may use such a phrase in connection with a case of incomplete individuation. I daresay you have not found your condition too inconvenient?"

"No, sir," said Marguerite. "On the contrary, it has had a strengthening effect upon me. I have never had a moment of loneliness in my life."

"You are a strong girl," the doctor conceded. "Well-shaped legs, splendid haunches—hold still, ninny, I'm merely palpating you. Do you think I'm like your salacious priest? Now, let me just get my hand in here between—"

"I advise you not to try that!"

"Why not? Good Lord, I have to find out the nature of the connecting tissues, to see if your guts are all mixed up together, or if it's just a flap of gristle and a few hairs."

"Be careful!" Marguerite warned him, flinching away. "She doesn't like that!"

"I'm not going to hurt either of you, damn it! Hold still!"

"Look out—I feel her moving! She moves only when she's going to bite!"

"She can't bite where I'm feeling. . . . Ugh!"

"Oh, Doctor! Doctor!"

"I'll be all right. Now, you stay right here while I wash up a bit. Stand as still as possible. I'll just take a squint at the manual, and—"

"Promise me that you won't hurt her!"

"I promise," the doctor said, and he went out of the closet, leaving the door slightly ajar.

Marguerite listened for the sound of knives being sharpened, was reassured by the gurgling of a heavy liquid being poured out of a bottle. Peeping out, she saw the doctor heating a beaker over his Bunsen burner. Suddenly he flung the door open and marched toward her, holding the beaker aloft. The miserable girl crouched in the corner, hiding her back from him.

"Now, now," the doctor said soothingly, "this isn't going to hurt much. It's nothing but castor oil which I have warmed slightly. Now stand up as straight as you can—out here, away from the wall."

Marguerite stood up as straight as she could, closed her eyes, and opened her mouth wide, prepared to swallow the whole beakerful of castor oil. Instead she felt it emptied over her head. The warm oil flowed swiftly down over her body, coating her evenly from head to foot. At the same moment the doctor outrageously tickled the little sibling where she could not bite. Little sibling moved slightly—a fateful move! Oil flowed for the first time between the intimate twins. Little sibling tried to move back, found her ancient grip untenable, the comfortable indentations slippery with oil. Faster and faster she moved—oh, what a scrabbling and grabbing of tiny claws, what a clicking of impotent teeth! Little sibling had lost her grip! Down, down, down she slid, into the abyss of insecurity, fighting so ferociously that it seemed at times as if she would surely regain her throne. Almost she succeeded in hanging a tooth into a shapely buttock, where she might in time have consolidated a mediocre position. A force even more inexorable than her will pulled her toward the center of the earth. Down those lovely legs, without a bristle to cling to, she flailed like a tiny helicopter settling to rest, unable to generate quite enough power to rise up through the air again. A treacherous viscosity, bland as a legal seduction, came between the two sisters, parted them, sundered them, foiled the passionate adhesion of their two skins. Down, down, down—*plop!*

The little sibling rocked uncertainly on her cowboy legs, panting, blinking slit-eyed up at the unscalable height. Then, with a crafty expression on her face ("If not the Peacock Throne, then—"), she darted mother-naked out of the closet, into the office, clutched up a handful of old bandages, and scuttled out of the building through a large rathole that the doctor had been meaning to fix. They heard her clucking as she encountered the snow.

"Oh—oh—oh! See what you've done!" Marguerite shrieked hysterically, reaching as far as she could into the rathole. It was with some difficulty that the doctor prevented her from bolting out into the snow in pursuit of the sibling.

"Don't worry," the doctor said. "She can take care of herself."

"No, she can't!"

"Here, towel yourself off with the rest of these bandages. What's good for the goose—"

"She knows nothing of taking care of herself!"

"You underestimate her. She is a keen observer of human nature. Drink this. Your problem will now be to keep from bending over backward."

As Marguerite reached her house at the edge of town, she saw the sibling disappearing over a hill. The clever creature had wrapped those old bandages about herself so that she looked exactly like a jolly little nurse who had just got off work and was out for a roaring good time. She was skipping along hand in hand with Paris, the beautiful stranger.

"She will soon get tired," thought Marguerite, scrubbing off the symbols the boys had chalked on her door as usual, but pausing for a moment over an especially interesting one. "She is really quite small. Perhaps he will let her ride piggyback."

Travels of Helen Medusa

It is generally recognized that human beings must avoid uttering Truth if speech is to continue. By universal agreement, Goodness is eschewed as deleterious to all other kinds of intercourse, including the serious one of perpetuating the race in order that it may continue to make money. The few who have shown tendencies not to conform to these wholesome precepts have been speedily punished by natural causes, that is to say, by the mere externalization of the inner conflicts that led them to speak Truth or practice Goodness, which are attributes of God and of God only. In respect of Beauty—the third of God's aspects—there have been fewer impostors. Their punishment has not always been of a kind that one would readily anticipate. . . .

A young poet came into his lodgings late one night and found there a woman waiting for him. She stood in the middle of the room, without moving. The poet trembled, for his heart had been broken by a woman the year before, when he was fourteen, and he did not wish ever to love again. He believed it was necessary to love in order to make love; so he was inexperienced in this kind of knowledge, though sophisticated in others, being a precocious youth. Now he trembled also with fear of the unknown; for this woman's face was concealed by a black veil so heavy that he wondered how she could see through it. The lines of her body were similarly masked. Although it was a warm spring night, and the scent of jasmine was in the air, she was

116

dressed as if for winter. Long, black gloves masked her hands; her shoes were old-fashioned high-topped ones that buttoned up the side. Yet everything about her was elegant with a timeless certainty of taste. She wore no perfume; but emanating from her motionless figure, in an inexplicable way, were a grace and dignity that she could not conceal; and it struck him that this must be the daughter of some ancient and noble house that did not change with the times.

"Who are you? What are you doing here?" he stammered, and though the words themselves were brusque, he uttered them with the quality peculiar to him, by which he gave everything an unprecedented expansion, and included himself as if he had no private interests, so that even his enemies were strangely melted by the poignancy of his hatred, and quickly sacrificed themselves to him in order to prevent his sacrificing himself to them without asking anything in return.

When the lady replied, her voice captured him with its splendor, although she spoke in a low tone, scarcely above a whisper, veiling her voice also:

"I come as a supplicant. Your poems have drawn me out of darkest dark, whence I thought never to emerge again. You are the opening of doors, beyond which I see the gods in all their joy. Take me in with you, poet! I give you my love, and I ask nothing of you except that you warm me for one moment!"

The poet leaned toward her. Taking her slender hand, he raised it to his lips; then he drew the glove off, although she tried at first to prevent it. He gasped at the beauty of that hand. Never had he seen such perfection. Quickly she hid her hand behind her.

"Oh, Lady, let me lift your veil!" he cried, and made as if to do so; but she backed away from him, affronted. "May I not see your face, then?"

"That you may not," she replied, "and I beg you never to ask me for reasons. If I tell you that it is better this way, will that not suffice—or is it too much for you to believe?"

"Nothing is too much for me to believe, Lady!" he said impetuously, shaking his head like a young bull, so that the black curls fell down on his forehead. "The existence of this world depends upon my belief, as you know, who have read my poems. I will never betray my sacred trust! I believe!"

"Then let our meeting be in darkest dark." She turned out the light.

So passed that night in darkest dark, and the boy, transformed into a man, found the joy of which he had had only furtive and scandalous premonitions, but which he knew to be comparable only to that canonization which he had foresworn along with the plan for suicide on a roller coaster. All future events of a similar nature, throughout his life, would unknowingly be based upon the impossible hope of recapturing the intensity of his existence at this moment, the time of his fall.

All his boyish dreams of metamorphosis through fiery excesses of love came true, all except one: He could not see the beauty of the beloved, and that seemed important to him, as he was a visual type. His fingertips could tell that she was lovely, but when they touched her face she seized them and kissed them or bit them tenderly, to make him willing not to stray further in that region. It was as if she was afraid he would discover some defect, some disfigurement that would make him recoil in horror.

Before dawn she dressed, swathing herself again so that she would remain invisible to the world. The boy flung himself at her feet, embracing her knees.

"Oh, my love, stay with me or I shall die! Do not leave me!"

"Do I mean so much to you, then, even though you cannot see me?"

For answer he bathed her hand in tears and, sinking to the floor, kissed every button on her shoes, feeling for them in the dark with his moist lips which, he would find, had come to resemble a red male flower during the night.

"Then I shall come again tomorrow," she said. "Go out as

usual and talk shop with your cronies until late at night. I shall be here when you return. Do not try to follow me. It will do you no good. Until then, beloved!" Suddenly she was gone.

"Oh, Lady, Lady! What is your name?" The poet rushed around the room, deliriously happy, yet tortured at the thought that she might not come back. If only he had some clue as to her identity or her appearance—aside from that hand that was so beautiful, the memory of it still hurt his eyes. Perhaps she was a very famous person—or perhaps someone he saw every day on the street. . . . Turning on the lights, he began to search for some object that she might have left behind. When he came to the bed, he could not contain himself, but leaped on it and rolled about like a lunatic, savoring the shadows of joy, the residue, the tracks and traces of love. It was as if he had tried to divest himself of everything physical. Suddenly he lay still and stared round-eyed. Among the shreds of his own dark, curling puberty, was a long, wavy golden hair. Glittering there like no other gold that ever was, it hypnotized him. Reverently he lifted it up, but not to the light, for it seemed to act like a prism, gathering light to it; then, like a philosopher's stone, it transmuted that light into gold on the spot. He could neither look at it for long nor keep his eyes off it. It excited him more unendurably than ever holy relic excited a martyr, or a halo a saint.

That day he could neither talk sense nor write poetry. He could do nothing but wander, roving the town, haunting the woods nearby, from time to time furtively glancing at the golden hair he carried wrapped around one finger, with a glove pulled over it. At his favorite tavern, early that evening, his appearance caused a sensation among his cronies, for whatever he felt always showed on his face in a form as exaggerated as the feeling itself, if not more so. "He is Apollo near death!" they cried, shielding their eyes. "Why does he come to disturb us with an insoluble prob-lem, when we have nothing but problems besetting us on every hand!" So they complained and joked, and were more than three-quarters serious, because the sight of him really hurt their eyes, although they were too polite to say so, in certain cases, and in other cases too vain to invite the imputation of weak eyes on account of the close work to which they were all committed. This time he did not even notice their clichés, upon whose detection depended his precarious livelihood—for although he was barely fifteen, many famous and elderly poets sat at his feet, all too thankful to receive a crumb of his innocent genius, which was universally acclaimed as quasi-divine.

When the time came, he ran to his lodgings, to find there his beloved waiting for him in darkest dark. There is no way to describe, without profanation, that which transpired, except to say abstractly that one does not improve on the supreme; in fact, one of the qualities of the supreme is its uniqueness; and yet, in its purest self, that is, so long as it is truly itself, it suffers no diminution in quality, extent, or duration. The course of a comet would be but an imperfect analogy.

On the nights that followed, it was always the same—she was there waiting for him, with the lights turned out, and only when they went to bed, in darkest dark, did she consent to remove the veil and all those other wrappings. Each night he reached for her face and got his fingers tenderly bitten, then licked by a little tongue that had the titillating virtues of a cat's tongue, guaranteed to reduce even a jaded old man to jelly—what, then, did it do to a precocious lad with no experience behind him, and no sense of proportion? Each night he would weep and beg to see her face— even if no more than a glimpse—and each night she would refuse, without tears, as if she would never be ready for tears, but always with profound melancholy.

"My love—oh, my love! Shall I never see you?" he groaned one night more passionately than usual; and he waited sulkily, lying there beside her, making his heart beat slower and slower until the rocking of the bed became almost imperceptible.

After a long silence she said in a voice heavy with sadness:

"You said that you would believe; but now, like the others, you must know. When you have seen my face, you can no longer love me."

"Oh, Lady, Lady! Let there be light between us! *You* shall also look upon *me*"—thus in his juvenile cunning he tempted her—"for I am more beautiful than Narcissus. My belly is a wisp of nebulae formed from the involuntary oglings of Apollo; my pectorals are the foreheads of fauns with the little horny bumps of Dionysus on them; my shoulders are the flights of Hermes at the Plutonian confines of our existence; my legs are curly brooks with the glimmering pallor which you have doubtless observed at dawn, when Eros and Eos cuddle together in the bed of Aphrodite. Here, put your hand here, and even here. Oh! Are you not happy? How can you wait to see me with your eyes? Or are you not a visual type?"

"I see you with my whole body," she mourned, "yes, and with my soul also. I love you, but do not speak of the beauty of famous people, for it is all too familiar to me. Name no more heroes— I want no more of them! All I want is you, for you are love, and all they are is courage, courage to slay and to make love, but not to love—not after they have seen me. Oh, poet, even you could not love me then!"

"You underestimate my abilities!" the poet cried recklessly. "Even though you are scarred and hideous and diseased, I will love you now and forever, for what is flesh but a veil, and what is life but a wonderful corruption in which the only sin is to keep oneself pure? No, it is *you* I love! Oh, my darling, a poet must see behind veils!"

"Choose, then, between loving and seeing," she said quietly.

"No, no!" he kissed her first upon one breast, then upon the other; then with his little finger and his thumb he spanned them, drawing them nearly together. "I cannot make that choice. It does not exist. If I say that the two are one, then they are one, even as you and I are one because I will it so. For this is *my* world, as you should know. I made it and I am constantly making it. If it is not right in any of its aspects, tell me and I will remake it. What have I overlooked in my haste? Ask anything of me, and I will make it for you. Beauty? Speak! Is it Beauty you want? But that is what I make better than anything else! It is my life, it is my work, the work I love best! Truth I make next best; and third, but not far behind, I make Goodness—for you, I will make it better than Truth or Beauty, if it is the want of that that saddens you."

"Your words are sweet, my poet," she said, and the music of her soft laugh made him soar into his own interstellar spaces even while he held her in his arms. "These things are the same, nor do I want them—oh, but I am tactless! Forgive me. Believe me, it is better—" Her reply was smothered by the kisses of the poet, whose generous heart embraced all defects, all uncouthnesses, and made them perfect with his love; for he needed ugliness even more than it needed him, even as another god needed chaos as raw material for another cosmos.

After a while her breathing told him that she was asleep, wearied with love. The poet's heart pounded with the fell purpose of the juvenile delinquent he would one day be. Slowly, cautiously he reached out, groped for the matches he had concealed in the ragged mattress. The match continued to burn until it scorched his fingers and went out; for there was no longer such an innocent set of reflexes in those fingers. As for his violet eyes, he would not know until dawn that they had become petrified.

At last he understood why she must walk veiled through the world, concealing her face from men—yes, and from women also, for they too are often easily affrighted by the abstract, to the extent that they cannot conduct ordinary transactions such as selling bread or wheeling a barrow or abetting a poor prostitute.

The poet shivered as if he had caught a stubborn chill from embracing the Second Law of Thermodynamics, immortalized in his poetry. The woman who lay there veiled in darkest dark had taken literally the teasing injunction of another prominent impersonator, to "be ye perfect." Fatal gaiety! She was a monster of perfection, inhuman as a star, static and self-contained as a perfect circle, a completeness that disfurnished the imagination of its duties and the heart of its privileges, forestalling the possibility and the desire to add to or to take away from or to alter even in the slightest. She was the most beautiful woman who had ever lived.

The one enormity, the criminal defect that the Creator cannot encompass or forgive is that perfection which renders his further existence pointless. With unfailing courtesy the poet, whose curly locks were now white as alum, assisted her in buttoning her shoes, after which he could not get up, but remained kneeling in darkest dark beside the open door, in an attitude of piety. Neither could he move his impotent tongue to say farewell. Helen Medusa did not expect statues to participate. Without a backward glance she resumed her journey.

THE PIOUS PUZZLES OF ANANDA MAHADEV

Ananda Mahadev Dattatreya was born near Srinagar in Kashmir on April 25, 1922, of a wealthy Brahman family. As he was intended for the priesthood, his family were glad to see the precocious boy become an adept at the spiritual discipline of yoga. They sent him for some years into the Ladakh region of Tibet as the chela, or disciple, of the great guru Hanuman Vikramaditya Mahasaya. In 1936 Sri Vikramaditya died as the result of austerities. Ananda spent the following two years traveling in Europe, Asia, and the Americas with his cousin, a worldly young man-about-Oxford. Although he studied for short periods at Oxford and the Sorbonne and for several years at Benares Hindu University, Ananda was incapable of much drudgery, so he never took an advanced degree. During World War II he enlisted in the British Army, fought in North Africa, and deserted while on leave, to serve under Subhas Chandra Bose in the national liberation movement of India. Christianity attracted him for some time, as did Zen Buddhism and the Brahmo Samaj sect, but he remained a devout Hindu to the end of his days. He was drowned in the Ganges at Benares, on June 12, 1953.

During my second sojourn in India I became interested in the personality—I might almost say the legend—of Ananda Mahadev. Although I never met him in the flesh, I was continually running into people whose lives had been affected by him. I still cannot completely account for his influence, which was sometimes good and sometimes evil.

Ananda was a man of extraordinary power that was generated, I daresay, by some kind of psychological conflict. He was gifted, learned, and young. Allowing for the tropical exuberance of his admirers, he also appears to have been rather a handsome man. This statement is corroborated by his friend Mr. P. A. Bruff, who provided me with a copy of the one photograph I have been able to find of Ananda. Presumably it was taken while he was drunk. The fulsome expression is said not to have been habitual. This is probably true in one sense, untrue in another. He alternated between periods of extreme asceticism and extreme abandon.

The fact that, through an unfortunate accident of nature, I am not insensitive to the occult, has led certain persons to suppose that I am some kind of apologist for it. Occult phenomena exist, but I do not know why they should. I dislike them strongly, for two reasons: (1) to the best of my knowledge, their only use is to supply superfluous evidence as to the unity of existence and the prevalence of life; and (2) they either complicate life by distracting us further, or they simplify it badly by offering a dubious escape. I wish to state now that I deeply regret the occult use that has been made of me. Had Ananda Mahadev not been lazy and disorderly, he would have written his own works while he was still on this side of Ganga Mata. I have other fish to fry, and it is characteristically unethical of him that he should not respect my separate identity. His reasons for choosing me are too complex to set forth here. With these words, which are my own, I shall have finished a task that, while not continuous, has nevertheless rendered uneasy more than a year of my life and has considerably impaired my health. At this point I care nothing for credibility.

I hope I have indicated that this work is the result of an enforced collaboration. The opinions expressed are not necessarily mine. The style is an unfortunate compromise. An example of his style is the title *Pious Puzzles*, which I leave untouched, in the spirit of rancor. It should have been *Religious Paradoxes*, of course. However, English is not his mother tongue.

Acknowledgments are due to Dr. Boris Wing and Dr. Aretino Scott, who helped me translate some of the notes from the Sanskrit in which Sri Ananda thought; to friends at Pendle Hill, who wish to remain anonymous, for help in editing the confused manuscript; and to the instigator of more than he knew, my beloved guru and Ananda's, the late Prabodh Chandra Bagchi of Santiniketan, "the Abode of Peace." *Shantih.*

i

The Monster

I shall never be the same since my encounter with the Monster.
He was sitting perfectly still.

Realizing that it was hopeless to escape, I danced about in my
fright, chattering at him, hoping to distract him from his purpose.

"How are you?" I said.

The Monster did not move or speak.

"Pardon me for such an arbitrary approach," I said. "I should
at least have given you a choice of questions. 'How are you?'
refers to the modality of your Being. Permit me to inquire into
your Being as such: *Who* are you?"

The Monster remained sitting perfectly still, not looking at
me with his eyes, but quite aware of me.

My hair stood on end. I was rooted to the spot. In that moment
I began to die—or rather I began to be like the Monster. Peace
stole over me.

Afterward someone who had grown up in the same country as
the Monster told me that he was not really much of a Monster
and that there was a real Monster at a certain place which was
not totally inaccessible.

"All the same," I said, "I know now what a Monster is, and that's
what I want to be."

ii

I was born to rule over principalities; instead I suffer privation.

Somewhere along the line the papers proving my right to rule were lost. They would have made my inheritance so easy! Instead of suffering as I do now, I should be served and treated with magnanimity.

I am so piqued at the loss of the papers that I am unable to show the infallible signs of noble birth which are also rightfully mine, namely, magnanimity and service.

iii

Ram's Report

A great examination is called. The examiner is formidable, not only because his command of data is unsurpassed, not only because he is an incomparable dialectician, but also because he is known to be animated by a spirit of contradiction. It is said that no one has ever been able to give him a satisfactory answer; therefore it is a question only as to the degree of one's failure. This degree of failure occasions the greatest anxiety to all candidates. I am taking the examination only as a lark.

Having considered the questions carefully, I am overcome by a feeling of lassitude. I hand in a blank piece of paper with my name in the upper right-hand corner. It is promptly returned to me, marked "100% correct! Bravo!" I let the paper fall listlessly to the floor, and walk out.

The examiner meets me at the door, shakes my hand, and asks me to be his assistant. I decline on the grounds that it might make complications. Then he offers to be my assistant. I thank him politely, and decline on the same grounds.

As I depart, I see the examiner pick up the paper I dropped, and begin to study it intently, bringing to bear upon it all the machinery of his vast intellect.

I shake my head sadly and wander off, wondering why I ever signed my name to the examination paper.

Hari's Report

Having spent more than thirty years preparing for the examination, was it any wonder that I faced it with dread? I did not so much fear that I should give the wrong answers—the examiner was a perfectionist and would mark everybody's answers wrong anyway. It was rather that I feared my inability to respond to some area of the examination—that it would remain simply a blank, an inconsistency I should have to make up at a later date, repeating the entire examination, and God alone knew when it would be offered again and whether I should really be any better prepared then than I was now!

That is why I had to complete the examination, to run the entire gamut of questions, and I assure you that it required more exercise of my faculties than you can easily imagine. The questions were purposely vague and disorderly, so that I should have to scent out the challenges myself, restate them, and make an incisive, systematic response, not so much to the particular question as to the whole subject.

It was with a certain modest self-esteem that I finally handed in to the examiner what I considered to be an authoritative, comprehensive treatise.

The examiner glanced at the first page, and, with a derisive gesture, marked the whole work with a big red zero.

As I dragged myself out of the room, I remembered, alas, too late, the technicality I had failed to observe. The papers were to have been handed in without any marks to identify the author, so as to ensure complete impartiality in the grading. And I—I had written my name as big as life, on the first page, in the upper right-hand corner!

For several years now I have been a candidate for reexamination, although I have received no official reply from the authorities. It may be that my earlier offers to sweep out the examination room and erase the blackboards after hours, were regarded as presumptuous, or perhaps even as intended to curry favor with the examiner.

In any event, I have been eagerly awaiting notices to the general public about the next examination. At that time, I fancy, some decision will have to be made on my case.

iv

Ram

I was sitting with some devotees in the temple of Vishnu, meditating in the profound silence, when I became aware of a rhythmical buzzing in my nose. How long it had been going on I did not know, as I am sometimes not fully aware of such things. I was sure that it must have been a considerable distraction to my neighbors.

I saw no remedy but to blow my nose. The noise reverberated so in the silence that I decided it would be better to confine the disturbance to one or two people than to annoy everyone, if the buzzing continued.

It continued. I tried holding my breath, but the obstruction in my nasal passages was so delicately attuned that the mere pulsation of the blood in my nose caused the buzzing to persist, though in a higher key and at a faster tempo.

I bowed my head in my hand in such a way as to be able to pinch my nostrils unobtrusively between my thumb and forefinger. Unfortunately the obstruction was located within the bony structure forming the bridge of the nose. I was unable to affect the rhythm of the buzzing sound.

At the risk of annoying my neighbors still more, I tried various other stealthy devices, all to no avail. I sat miserably until the end of the period of worship. At the first signs of general movement, I bolted.

As I stood leaning in exhaustion against the wall surrounding the temple, I suddenly realized that the buzzing had ceased. People began coming out of the temple. Just as I was leaving, the man who had sat next to me now fell in step with me. We looked into each other's eyes. Again I heard the buzzing sound.

All at once I realized that the location of the noise was not in my nose at all, but in his.

Hari

A memo on Puja worship at the temple of Vishnu last week. As soon as the silent meditation began, I noticed that the fellow next to me was making a distracting little noise with his nose. I might have accustomed myself to it, but he kept fidgeting and making efforts to stop buzzing. It was quite irritating.

I shall be careful not to sit by him again.

v

Ram's First Dying Statement

I am a man about whom everything is known, because I am wholly impure, and impurity is the one thing with which everybody is familiar.

In confessing this impurity, I hope to gain favor from myself. In confessing that I do this, I hope to gain still higher favor from myself. And so on, and on. Credit is my game.

But what is it that tirelessly turns favor to ashes in my mouth? It is not I, surely. If it were I, I should simply respect myself according to my desperate desire; but when I try to respect myself I lose all self-respect. . . . I am this persistent and inevitable corruption, and this going-beyond.

Am I? Am I this sailing? I am all of this except the Act itself. This Act propels me through the knowable into the pure Act of Being. It is the uncreated element in the soul; it is the true referent and taskmaster of my discontent, leading me from confession to confession, until all shall have been laid bare—as pure Act.

Hari's Second Dying Statement

I am a man about whom nothing is known, because there is too much to know about me and no point of departure for knowledge, any more than there is a conclusion.

You cannot begin by saying, "In the first place," because that is any place and no place, and both indications are equally mistaken. I myself do not know where I begin, although this is not to say that I do not know my own mind.

Nor could I help you with a definition, if I would. Place a form on me, and I evanesce to its opposite. Indict me as a devil, and I agree with you and am thereby an angel. Glorify me as an angel, and I agree with you and am thereby a devil. And I am always agreeing with you. . . .

Suppose I were to disagree with you? Would not that be a difficulty? Well, I must tell you, not in order to *make* the difficulty, but simply to state the truth, that I do disagree with you, and not just sometimes, but all the time.

It is not that I wish to elude you. I do not. It is your fault. You avoid me.

An agreement between us is impossible. I have had the experience of men humiliating themselves to death in order, seemingly, to agree with me, and I have almost sighed at the futility of it.

Dying is not enough. Indeed, you annoy me when you die, since you are merely trying to work on my sympathy. It can not alter your position. Right is right and you are wrong, and it will ever be thus.

I have already made up my mind about you; and what I think is Reality. There are no two ways about it. You do not seem to understand this.

You will pardon my seeming asperity, since this pardon will not involve you in any decisive change, and no good can come of it except that you will have exhausted one more irrelevancy. The more of this, the better. You have a long way to go before your dying can be said to count for anything.

As I have said, I know my own mind. I have also said that you will never understand me. You wonder, then, at my patience? All I can say is, it brings good results. However, this also surpasses your understanding.

I am a man about whom nothing is known.

i

I address myself to those who have botched their lives, are botching, or will botch them. It only awaits discovery that you are addressed.

Events address you. These words merely note your ruin.

Now that you are ruined—

ii

You tend to place the value of grief much higher than that of comfort? That is to make a false opposition. It is like saying that the frosting is better than the cake, when we shall be poisoned in any case.

Love the world. It is hard to overestimate its importance to the achievement of innocence.

iii

So long as there is life, there is no hope. Fortunately, our capacity for dying is limited only by the Absolute.

iv

These scabrous happenings are not accidents. Everything is important. When I am not simply grounded in Brahman, I am myself a wretched accident—unnecessary, without Being.

Brahman summons me by all sorts of events, from my apostasy. I cannot forget him for long.

There were many years in which I pretended not to know his language—when in reality it was the only language I did know.

v

The basic continuum of Reality is that Love which is so universally concerned for us that it lures and presses us from non-existence, through existence, into full Being—in Love itself.

vi

We are not spoiled or blighted for nothing. Whatever produces real agony must be affirmed even in our opposition, for man does not become aware without agony. Love stops at nothing to bring us into Being. (It even requires us to be zealously partisan in the alleviation of suffering, which has no meaning or interest except to Love.)

Under the strain of strength, we break into the dimension of weakness. Lying there, wholly supine, we acknowledge Reality as that which possesses us. In the virginity of our weakness, in the weakness of our virginity, out of the real strength of our Possessor, we are born again in strength.

Limitations exist to be broken. We clamp them upon ourselves, and, with agony and joy, we rend them from us.

Peace and Freedom are battle-scarred.

vii

Karma—the Language of Events—is the medium of our real education.

If I place myself beyond accident, I place myself beyond pain, and that is not a good in itself; for Brahman manifests his will most vividly in pain, and to know that one is in pain is to know that one is undergoing a mysterious change for which one would not have had the courage without him. If he does not always allow us to decline real pain, it is because the alternative is decay and death. The conservative man, the man who feels most secure, is in the greatest danger of all: the man who runs no risk runs the supreme risk.

Of one thing we may be certain in our present circumstances: There can be no real change without anguish, and no real anguish without change, although it may be for the worse, according to our karma. We may shudder with pain at the prospect of pain, but we must affirm it as an omen of survival. It is through pain that we are what we are—that our identity has been established in Reality.

viii

Pain is not disease; it is the indispensable symptom of disease. It does not drive us to distraction; it makes us aware of our distraction. Pain is the concentrator.

It is the liveliest directive we have toward Brahman, and the most concrete token of his continuous attentions.

As for me, I have always taken great pains to avoid small discomforts.

ix

The effect of our agonies is to place us in a wholly new and unfamiliar situation, that situation of pure possibility which we call the Unknown: it is unimaginably terrifying, and if we fully realized that we were arriving in it, the uttermost depths of our cowardice would be stirred and our agonies would be greatly increased.

If we knew all the facts, we should never dare move even one little finger of our own accord. We should prefer not to be born. It is only the will of Brahman, personally overriding our abject conservatism, that makes us do interesting things, or (as we would complain in the midst of our agonies) plunges us into the most reckless and hair-raising adventures imaginable.

There is a boast to which man is entitled, yet he does not make it, for fear he will be put to the test—as if it were not proved at every moment of his life. The boast is: There is nothing I cannot endure.

x

When we say that our capacity for anguish is limited, we are also saying that our capacity for change is limited. There *are* limits, but it is not we who state them, but events. When we state them, we are trying to play a bargaining game.

xi

"My heart is filled with its own reasonings, perfect and impenetrable. Thou canst not enter!"

And the Reply comes:

"I will break thy heart."

xii

Virtue is in greatest danger when it begins to bring good results. There are habitually virtuous men, but there is no habitual virtue.

Rather: At certain points in History, the soul of man is so wrung by ghastly and unimaginable anguish that, with a gesture of loathing, it tears off its own flesh—the livery of Existence itself—and rushes into pure Being, where it confronts—Almighty God. And with a terrible voice it cries out:

"My God! My God! Why did you do it?"

And God looks on him with eyes of infinite love, and parting his own robe, shows lacerations that duplicate exactly those suffered by man's soul.

And God says:

"Art thou not here?"

"Lord, *why?*"
"So that thou mayest have Freedom and Myself."
"Lord, I would be satisfied with thee."
"Man, I would be satisfied with thee."

✦❀✦❀✦❀✦❀✦❀ *The Ocean of Maya*

i

The Ocean of Maya is a fellow creature, a fellow pilgrim and passenger. It blindly, accidentally, involuntarily spawns up, sea-changed (how else?), whatever Fate has cast into it, and thereafter it laves and loves for it as no other element can ever do. That force is to be respected, appeased by sacrifice, made use of as it blindly desires. . . .

The mature man encompasses the sea—and the land and the heavens—in the widenesses of his soul. Stern or jovial, he is serenely so. With the decorum of Sankara and Ramanuja, with the dignity of Zeno and Epicurus, he holds steadfastly apart the curtains of his soul, and the spaciousness of him is godly beyond belief. But when those curtains drop, nothing may be seen but a scurrying rat.

ii

Mata Maya, Maya Mata, I cannot change you, for you are the Ocean that has worn me into my curious form. But I can assert my independence of you, and I can endure through time, and I can triumph over you through the love that descends like the rays of Surya from above, and in that way meet (though you will never understand how or why) the fateful tides and undertows of your love for me. And I pray Vishnu to still my soul so that this

142

love, this charity, this pity, this understanding, and this whole affirming can be.

iii

I walk by the always turbulent surf. It makes a good rhythm for my nerves and passions to jump to, offers a pertinent orthodoxy of nature, as it were, to legitimize the involuntary and distressing orgy that I am. Then I must bow before the amplitude of this passion of which I partake "supremely with respect to the self." Of the inner surf, as of the surf of the Ocean Stream, I am not asked to approve. The question is, rather, What are the conditions under which *it* can be prevailed upon to approve of *me?* . . . Sea stones, shells, and old bottles wouldn't *like*, if asked, to suffer their sea-change, but they suffer it anyway and come to resemble me.

There begins, perhaps, in the appreciation of the surf in which we live and have our being and struggle to breathe—and do breathe—in the affirmation of it in a vision of creation—there, I say, begins perhaps that dimension of philosophic calm, our most royal heritage, the prelude—what else could it be?—to human wisdom.

iv

I am always in a passion. Sometimes I am merely simmering; at other times I am boiling and heaving and churning like an internal-combustion engine—my brains throb, my guts are the Laocoön, and my heart and lungs, howlingly hideous, devour each other—and all is miraculously reconstructed like Prometheus's liver. Then I want to die because it is all so horrible, so disorderly—in short, so trying. Things are too interesting and they do not fulfill my wishes. . . . The spectacle, the richness, the variety are almost too much for me. Nevertheless, I have a gauge to my endurance. It is that which has always kept me from extending myself too far beyond my powers; that which has

always made me come up for air, out of the effluvium of anxiety
and dread; that which makes me get atop of it somehow, though
perhaps only at the point where it has ridden me into the dust.
And this is a law that I have tested and been saved by many a
time. It is the most reliable thing about me, because it is not mine.

v

The human being is like a boulder, filled with the violent sub-
stantive life of rock, a form shoaled up out of inward infinity,
taking its place in the continuous upheavals and transformations
of outward infinity, and all is one unbroken process in which
"outward" and "inward" have no meaning except as experi-
mental inventions of the process itself.

Our speech expresses our experience as fumes express the chemical changes of inorganic substances. Silence also is the expression
of a state of being. Visualize the mysterious effluvium that ema-
nates from stars, boulders, and other inorganic masses: It is a mere
extension of the turbulent process within.

So with the human voice. It reflects, responds to, participates
in the intense activity of the organism of which it is a part. In
this effluvium of speech are shoaled up forms, passions, reasonings.
Among its ceaseless metamorphoses a system of thinking is seen,
like the hull and ribs of an ancient Chinese junk in the sand of
Lanka, partially exposed by the waves. It is heaved up, then folded
under, to be seen again or not, but never in the same form. And
the gibbering and the chattering, character assassination and sage
advice, responsible and irresponsible speech—how could it be
otherwise? An infinitely various, electrifying, dream-bearing, irritating, nourishing medium of the human soul, it *can not cease*
so long as the human soul continues to live and to evolve, churning up for its own discovery, out of its infinite depths, nothing
less than all the nuances of all the modalities of the relative universe.

In the beginning was the Word.

vi

As mysterious as the words of monkeys is the saying, Knowledge is power. Knowledge is identical with power, but what do we know?

From our infancy, and even before birth—who knows how long before?—all the impulses of the world sink into the inner distances of our sphinx-like depths.

Our outer minds are only tumbling flashes, traces of the bottomless interior which has unforgettable knowledge of all creation, and which is bound forever to reenact the process of creation.

Consider the unaccountable depths of sleep that we carry with us even in the brightest day, over the highest hurdles of thought—thought so lofty that only its own experience has reality to it. . . . We are mostly asleep, and at night we are altogether asleep. But night sleep is not suspension; it is a resolute plunge into universal subjectivity, to which we cease to object, and in which creative, turbulent order we revel, until we are expansive enough to face again the attritions of objectivity. . . .

vii

It is impossible to act as we wish, that is, decisively, without further entanglements or consequences, for all time. If it were possible to act in this way, it would never be necessary to act again. That is, of course, what we wish. We desire nothing short of the pure, eternal Act of Being. That is, we are not satisfied with anything short of Brahman.

viii

Now I will tell thee what the will of God is. The will of God is that every man realize in himself the entire range of human experience, in a mighty and protracted struggle for God himself. It is the will of God that man will God, just as it is the will of man that God will man. Neither can compel the other. Their powers of persuasion are limited, for their languages are constantly changing, like everything else—changing to fit change. Because of his freedom, man is as mysterious and unpredictable to God as God is to him. It is a unique and passionate affair. Even if one party suffered a loss of interest, neither could honorably withdraw. It would be dangerous.

ix

I have no virtue, but only a human characteristic which is inseparable from vice—that of mobility: The same mobility that allows me to seek Brahman also allows me to fall into snares and pitfalls.

But this mobility is not merely neutral: The proclivity to risk is a part of it, and "only risk is not fatal." Every vested interest of the soul will keep it stationary while ever-present doom descends on it. And yet this doom of the old must precede the birth of the new.

Before a man can be born again, a severe and purifying crisis is required, in which the old rigid terms of the ego are wholly exhausted, bankrupted, and buried. It is the exhaustion of finite individual existence.

The danger lies in the obsessive and failure-destined attempt to reconstruct the same old ego, only more strongly, of course, and therefore more provocatively than before. And the Lesson, which is our despair and our hope, will be repeated until it is learned—or until pride closes fast the book of the soul.

x

We live, we rove, we inhabit the spheres of process, too weak for anything but change. We cannot bear to repeat even one single combination of events. So long as we have patience not to learn, the one Lesson will be repeated. . . .

xi

To be as patient with the will of God as he is with our dis-obedience—that is to establish a *modus vivendi*.

xii

We shaved this morning to uncover our expression. It was there all right, and in the discovery. We greeted each other with relief.

The extreme loveliness of childhood is to tell us with mytho-logical simplicity that we are created in the image of Brahman. Gradually this pure surface is obscured by fadings and hollow-ings, by hair and by complex lines of personality. There is nothing sudden in the change. We are given all the time in the world. The stages are minutely graded so that we can see the image more and more in depth, experimenting as we go.

Slowly, deliberately, and with great indulgence the image is effaced inward by degrees, layer by layer, toward the central reality. Much depends on our attention and cooperation at all times (although the meaning of the whole process can dawn on us at any point in our education): for the image is going to be dispensed with altogether, and the present demonstration will come to an end.

xiii

Society and the individual do not wait for each other. When one is ripe for revolution, the other can go hang, and there has never been a retraction in all of history.

God speaks any time, and the most likely time is the most un-likely, and the most unlikely is the most likely.

xiv

Brahman created man, but does not manipulate him. This is the supreme test of his love for man and of man's love for Brahman.

And it is because of the grandeur of this eternal decision that evil exists for us.

On the other hand, the pressure of circumstance—the Language of Events—forces man to make decisions about his own destiny. Events are always questioning him, and, willingly or unwillingly, he is always having to make an answer. He is usually unwilling.

xv

Some men are like big luminous fish that move swiftly and momentously through the depths of the ocean, but when they are hauled to the surface they are blind and clumsy, and even the tiniest minnow is safe in attacking them. Their explosions are of interest to haruspice, sortileger, analyst.

xvi

Great names lie on us like acid.

xvii

A study of the achievements of great men invariably reveals defects which disprove popular opinions as to their perfection. Such revelations of the shaky foundations of our civilization lead to such alarm at the absence of any true authorities, that one grasps the wretched materia of humankind, with irreverent, workmanlike hands, determined to do things better, to make things stronger, keener, purer, more authoritative. Why, civilization is so shaky that *everyone* is needed to hold it together. Even I am needed!

xviii

When a man accomplishes a great work, it does not mean that the prohibitive is not demanded of him also.

xix

Everything in life is bent upon the destruction of our individuality; therefore it is necessary to define oneself as an individual.

We may well be relieved because it is so consistently perilous. But those who come to depend on this (for them) artificial peril develop no further.

XX

Every experience is great and mysterious. May we respect it as if it were a god walking among us in the guise of a casual stranger.

Painful Possibilities

i

"He knocks outside. Our opening and his entry are simultaneous." Anxiety and disaster are also simultaneous.

ii

To be present is to offend; to be absent is to offend; to be present and absent is to offend.

Finally, not to offend is to offend. There is no alternative to offense. Therefore offense is unthinkable.

iii

One might put it this way: The things you desire are the things you do not have, and the things you fear are the things that do not have you.

If you desire a continuation of the things you have, it is the continuation—which you do not have—that you desire. If you fear a continuation of the things that have you, it is the continuation—which does not have you—that you fear.

iv

Go to the slug, thou ant heap. Consider his ways. . . . The slug can sit still. He keeps cool and calm; he takes no thought for the morrow. All is provided for him. When he moves, it is an event. A carpet is laid down to commemorate his pleased and effortless passage.

v

The passage of time has ambivalent meaning for man. He is at once subject to regret at the loss of an irrevocable and unique series of possibilities, and to relief at having survived them. He is consumed by remorse at not having acquitted himself well enough, and he has a sense of progress at having passed beyond the reach of specific situations of a dubious and indecisive character. Between these two conflicting values, man exists in continuous present anxiety, emigrating into the unknown and transforming it into the known, from which he is a refugee.

Man escapes continually: by the skin of his teeth; by the grace of God; by the overcomplicated structure of the world trap, which is always springing itself too soon, or getting in its own way and trapping a part of its own mechanism.

Man escapes. What is caught is not man, but only an arm, a leg, and so on. He escapes thus because he is man, and he is man because he escapes thus.

⊷⊱⊷⊱⊷⊱⊷⊱ *Dying by Hand*

i

Life is a crisis of Death. For a short time Death looks down the muzzle of existence, but he does not quite pull the trigger. Then, his nerve shaken, he drops the revolver and goes on as before—as before that unpardonable intensification of non-existence during which he had a most harrowing vision of activity.

ii

If a man takes the position of being alive, then let him take it firmly, without hesitation or reservation. He has rejected the position of being unreservedly dead, because he could find no degrees of death; similarly, there are no degrees of life. If he is to escape the accusation of shilly-shallying, he must affirm wholly the position of being wholly alive. Such an affirmation may entail heroism. No matter, it is natural.

iii

From the time we are born we begin to run out roots in all directions, as far as possible, and to interweave them into the soil of life, to suck our substances from it. We suppose life comes to expect this enterprise from us, as a vast system of commitments. That is what makes it so hard to die. When we think of dying, we think of the effect death would have in each commitment. If we are too entangled to live, we are also too entangled to die.

iv

We try to bind others to our service and to cut their ties with the world—instead of binding ourselves to their service and cutting our own ties with the world.

v

We want each other to be sick. It gives us confidence that we are needed.

We want each other to die, so that we can make a fresh start.

We want things to be very young, very old, very exotic, sick, or dead. They are less of a problem than those who, like ourselves, are like ourselves.

vi

Brahman weakens us here, strengthens us there; here he heaves us up out of not-being, there he ducks us down into nothingness—now speeding it up, now slowing it down, making it dark, making it light. Does all this seem accidental to you? This seeming is no accident.

vii

Madness is the feeling that we can not love until we have time. We shall never have time until we love.

viii

Sometimes we are so intent upon practicing love, that we hate those who interrupt us. Why should we have to *apply* the damned thing?

ix

In your exhaustion you are disturbed because you lack sufficient strength and collectedness to overcome your lack of sufficient strength and collectedness. A tautology.

This exhaustion is a fine thing. In it you will learn to do without strength and collectedness. You will dispense with vitality and you will dispense with reason; but you will go on, not doggedly but simply, in a state of ultimate capitulation.

There is evidently more than one way of dying. The world helps to kill us; but we must learn to cooperate by exhausting ourselves through our own inner contradictions—if we have not already learned it. If we choose this way, we must be ready for the death each time it occurs—for we are cowards and we must die many times.

By being ready, I mean that we should make sure that we are really wiped out, and are nothing but standing invitations to Life.

x

Choices based upon self-interest are not to the true interest of the self, except insofar as they aid in bringing about a crisis.

xi

Brahman gives us what we want, particularly if it will make us sick.

xii

The atmosphere is important to the candidate for Being; but he should not remain too long among the athletic of spirit. He must expose himself continually to disease, or his health is hollow.

Health is no less contagious than disease; but it is possible to build up a fatal immunity to either.

xiii

Life offers no challenge; rather, man is a porcupine, offended and offending.

A man can only be hurt when he is full of the *maya* of his own importance. In emptying himself of himself, he must be absurdly incautious. If he makes the slightest reservation, nothing happens. If he so much as plucks at a thread on the sleeve of his departing ego, the whole ego remains.

If he takes hold of one blade of grass, the world stops in its tracks.

xiv

When the little light died, it knew then that the big darkness was a light so bright that it was darkness to the little light.

◆《◆《◆《◆《◆《 *An Inner Quailing*

i

      I have always been a fool. Ever since I first cracked the dawn with the unforgivable insolence of an ego shriek, I have desisted from folly only long enough to assert that I was a fool.

My life—the less said about that, the better. Not once have I succeeded in thinking of nothing.

This is not to say that I have not frequently been lucid.

ii

Brahman has endowed me with the feeblest powers of concentration, presumably so that I should not be able to ignore anything. This shows on his part an admirable realism which is not generally recognized. . . . Suppose you had written a poem, and some mad fool were to become so enamored of a particular figure of speech that he threatened to die before reading the rest of the poem—not that he could ever really get to the bottom of it. Would it not make you furious?

iii

      To learn that one is not particularly bright, not uncommonly gifted with imagination, unwise, wild, not very kind, impatient, easily bored, rather blind, not especially sensitive, unworthy of prolonged attention—to learn these things about oneself is to be at a great advantage in terms of humility.

Great pride is then possible.

iv

What is the difference between repentance and chagrin? Between humility and humiliation?

The confession of venial sins may fill one with mortal pride.

v

We are so readily duped, flimflammed, fleeced, skinned, hoodwinked, and deceived, that we can only conclude that there must be some force in us which distrusts the virtue of prudence.

Speaking for this force, a voice says: We should deliberately allow ourselves to be duped. Otherwise we might have too serious an influence on events—an influence that would be conservative, intelligent, and disastrous.

vi

When a man discovers Brahman, it is Brahman who makes the discovery. When Brahman is not discovered, it is man who has failed again.

vii

It is necessary to avoid perfection. The perfect saying does not communicate. It does not offer that possibility for misunderstanding which releases us from the absolute tension of opposites and the obligation to capitulate absolutely. Man is not ready for this.

The hint, the innuendo, the rumor of perfection—that is the process by which men grapple together and grow. That is the secret of the Vedas.

It is possible, speaking slowly, clearly, and with utmost simplicity, to say absolutely nothing.

viii

Do not scoff at the impurity of those who are capable of pointing to perfection—as if you were exposing a secret flaw which nullified whatever they might say or do about perfection.

On the contrary, it is the tragic flaw, the mask of humanity which alone gives man the authority and the reason for speaking of Brahman.

In olden times, who was it that the noble maidens and young men consulted on the consummation of marriage? The eunuch.

ix

Lastly, there is the purification by nonachievement. Again, the Event speaks the word—a terrible volcanic upheaval, the draining of an ocean, and the basic condition is established for the gradual, painful development of a civilization whose entire etymology refers to that Event.

Purification by nonachievement begins by what we think is some inconsistency of the Process. That is, it begins as failure in the external world, through some inner quailing. Actually, it is no inconsistency at all if it leads to failure, for the realization of failure is the radical purpose of the Process. It is the realization of Process itself, and it places us at once beyond Process.

Failure is our only hope, and weakness our only virtue. But we are not safe in our weakness, even after failure. The sudden path from Process is also the sudden path back to Process. To *visualize* oneself as that pure act of Being is once again to objectify oneself as a part of the Process, but now as an *invidious* part, so that one is far worse off than before; for he is now both proud, and deluded as to his true condition.

It is only when one cannot regard the pure act of Being as an achievement, that one may be said to have attained nonachievement. One is then that pure act of Being.

The bird of paradise alights only upon the hand that does not grasp.

i

In the flung gift of the brigand lies love; refuse it at his peril. The cutthroat murders on his knees; the rapist is hopelessly in love with God.

The criminal says: "You know that I am not my deeds, my words, or my thoughts. I demand that you love *me!* Now—your love or your life!"

The fallacy of his argument lies in the assumption that we can give one without the other.

ii

It is natural for him to attack when he cannot defend. Indeed, it is his defenselessness that compels him to attack, or suffer an irreparable victory.

iii

He is impatient to set things right before his doom, and it is precisely impatience that has made things wrong.

iv

To refrain from peeking when he is in a position to change his mind—that is tact.

v

Do I wish him well? No, I wish him ill. I wish him the worst thing imaginable to him: A change of his identity. . . . His death would not satisfy me, because that would merely terminate, not solve, the problem of him. It would merely break off the relation between us, and as he disappeared, his hateful face would be grinning at me—"*Au revoir!*" I could hardly consent to that, could I? So I have to be involved with him, to change him—and by the same act, be changed by him. Then, you say, love might occur. Very well, let it. I would pay even that price in order to be rid of him.

vi

The struggle is too great to be confined to this hour. I see now that it will have to go on the whole day regardless of what I seem to be doing—and all night and all day tomorrow and the next day—on and on. . . .

Suppose I were to win? I should then have to take the initiative in another struggle, until I succeeded in being defeated.

No, victory is the one embarrassment I could not endure. It would be pure Hell.

Sometimes it is necessary really to forget how to fight—even when such a forgetting is not a technique of fighting; for otherwise one might win, and the prize would be—forever lost!

vii

To have peace with the enemy, we must evacuate the areas coveted by him. It is necessary to evacuate the world.

But it is ignoble of us, and understandably irritating to the enemy, that we should force him to demand the world. We should have offered it to him before he ever thought of wanting it.

When did he first begin wanting it? As soon as it became evident that we were seriously occupying it as if it belonged to us.

The objection is made that it is too late to disengage ourselves from the position that we have taken—that the enemy can never forgive our churlish behavior, and that we must now fight for our lives.

Hence the question is now, Is it possible to relinquish the world, as we wish, or must our fear that we cannot, always constitute a threat of war?

viii

To prevent war, we must give the enemy what he wants before he wants it—that is, before he is an enemy. We must try to anticipate his desires. Better yet, we should not in the first place put ourselves in the position of one who is capable of granting or withholding possessions; for the granting of favors can be more embarrassing to the recipient than the withholding of them.

And now the enemy is at the door, demanding the love we have withheld. If we open at this late date, we run the risk of being ravished to our heart's content.

While we are piling the furniture against the door, we shall think of the idyllic days of our self-esteem and it will give us the courage to hang ourselves—for there is no risk involved in that.

ix

Evidently it is too late to escape with our lives. The world is not enough. We must make the supreme sacrifice, in order to convince the enemy and ourselves that we really love him. In fact, we cannot really love him *until* we are dead.

Well, that's how matters stand. We are in the wrong and the enemy is in the right—he is always right, confound him. He will never leave us in peace until we love him; but then, of course, he will never leave us.

x

When you feel yourself being defeated, exterminate yourself. Otherwise the charge of obstinate warmongering may be added to all the rest.

The time for death should be selected with extreme care. All the resources of empirical observation and intellectual judgment should be used; but deliberation is not enough. Quick intuition and passion should be given free rein until they culminate in dream-sure conviction. One should not enjoy suicide too soon; nor, certainly, should one delay too long, lest the enemies become so formidable that one is unable to disengage oneself.

xi

The entire struggle has been precipitated and maintained by our stubborn declaration of independence, our assertion of the right to live our own life. But at this point, after so many years of bloody and protracted warfare, why are we unable to agree to armistice terms, let alone a treaty?

It is because of the enemies within the gates, the real profiteers, the secret third side who depend upon war—who brought about the declaration itself. The enemy without would come to terms gladly, having fewer commitments, or rather less binding ones, with our profiteers, than we do. But cessation of war would mean the death of our profiteers as such—they are in it too deeply to get out alive. As are we.

In order to exterminate the warmongers as such, we must ruin ourselves. We are then, as it were, an open city, dead in the sense that our leaders, arrogant with war-given powers, are dead. Henceforward we participate only modestly in world affairs. It is our afterlife. We are at peace, and our presence is felt only as peace. If we had enjoyed suicide earlier or later, it would not have been the same.

xii

There is only one way to resist the pressure of present slaughter, and that is to do absolutely nothing. It is not possible to reject the flux of matter over the nerve ends except by abandoning the fight in terms of nerves—by allowing the contamination of the world bath: a contamination which will be complete and toxic if we thresh about, inactive if we capitulate.

Even Brahman does not war with matter on its own terms.

Passive resistance alone is possible—that is, it may have partial, sporadic success. On the corrupt level of mere existence it is impossible to remain intact. Only capitulation to Existence can liberate us to Being.

Close the orifices of the body to matter, tighten your pores to the wind, resist—and you will be tortured and killed, without legal recourse, for the body is wedded to matter. Pretend virginity and you suffer real rape.

xiii

I am the king, the crown, and the throne. I am the carpet and the court. I am the jester, and I am the cap and bells.

I am the neighboring state and the territory in question. I am the tension and the war. I am defeat and I am victory, death and life, you and I.

All of this is seeming, and I am this also.

xiv

Pardon all before you understand all, or you will not understand or pardon.

Pardon your neighbor before you forget the offense.

xv

It is the eleventh hour.

The burden is altogether upon us. We are absolutely responsible, although victory can never be ours. We can be blamed for failure, but we can never take credit for success. The best that can be said of us is that we may have surrendered.

Actually the clock strikes nothing but twelve, though in a variety of ways. The variety is supposed to afford us comfort. Why are we so uncomfortable? Because the variety is the completed logic of the argument that hems us in from every possible angle. It leaves us no loophole. We are inextricably caught in the monotony of complete variety.

It is twelve o'clock.

Teetering

i

We are as miserable as possible. Reason keeps us from getting any worse or any better. We shall never stand in greater need of escape than we do at this moment. There is no improvement, no progress, only a worsening—short of the leap. Conditions are always ideal.

In the evolution of species, it is the sudden, extreme, and illogical act—the mutation—that places a new creature in a new environment. The old species, confident of slow, gradual progress, remains in the old environment, increasing in size and prestige, exactly like the dinosaurs in the swamp.

ii

Alas, nothing is so simple as simplicity, or so simple to find. One does not achieve it; one accepts it, or rather falls heir to it, as to a contested legacy. All that is required is the exhaustion of alternatives.

iii

The mind may develop the most stunning and precise of metaphysical systems; but such objective heroisms remain abstract, even though the problem of subjectivity is their study.

"Decisiveness inheres in subjectivity alone," in substantial transcendence and independence of philosophy; but the latter is presupposed just as man's fallen state is presupposed by salvation. Indeed, philosophy is precisely the formulation of man's fallen state.

It is the difference between the study of embryology and the experience of birth. Or, more exactly, it is the difference between analysis and regeneration.

And, speaking of mental heroism: Was there ever heroism without risk? Philosophy is a discipline that prepares a man for a blind leap. *Philosophia ars moriendi*. Suppose the leap is not made? In that case, another preparation would have done as well and as badly.

iv

There is nothing to recommend Being, because there is no transition from Not-Being. There is no bridge, no logical connection with our everyday life, with Philosophy, Science, or Common Sense. From none of these can you see your way, nor can the way be demonstrated to you. You will balk at the very first step, which is hair-raising. . . . You cannot walk cautiously into Being; you must leap in pitch darkness.

No one is going to push you, nor is the ground going to crumble suddenly beneath you. You would like that all too well. You court danger, sauntering carelessly along the edge of the abyss, turning your back on strangers. . . . Nothing is going to happen.

But no one is going to call you back, either.

✶✦✶✦✶✦✶✦✶✦ *Telecommunications*

i

I speak to the innumerable faces of the One. As I say good morning to you, I mean I love you, and my hair stands on end and my knees tremble, and I would fall down and worship you if I were not afraid of offending you by seeming not to be united with you—if I were not afraid of seeming to think of you as a thing limited by my separate existence. And indeed I surely offend you in being excited by you as by some particular thing, some mere manifestation of you.

My consciousness of these considerations is a menace to our unity. Indeed, my consciousness is the ultimate menace. Only my death can satisfy your honor.

I am not worthy of this noble race. Will go forth. Solitude of a tree or cave. Finish the grisly exploit, mean, without charity, love reversed by the demand for love. Will return after death, absolutely general. Presence felt then only as a gracious affection.

ii

When there is no referent but the Absolute, one is quite safe in contradicting oneself. No one can ever be unhinged whose door is off altogether.

That creaking noise? To be a sound, it requires both the movement of hinges—and your ear.

iii

I make no communication. I am this simply, though in process. To make communication is to question the fact of that perfect communication which I am. It is to attempt to make a substitute for Reality.

I do not make love to you, because that is to deny the fact of our perfect union—that union which is our Being.

And yet, because we are in process, I communicate my love to you. To communicate this is to communicate the fact of my redundancy. If you see this, process has been justified. Otherwise, not.

iv

We speak the language of those whom we address. And whom do we not address?

v

If my speech is odd, it is not so odd as your waywardness. My words are not wild; they faithfully follow your leaping. The actions of divinity are asterisked by the embarrassing disorder of the constellations.

vi

You say that my arguments are beyond reason. Worse, you now state that they also lack the irrefutable charm of nonsense— that there simply is no communication between us!

I reply: Only in pure unity is there no communication.

vii

We must be clear about that which is finally obscure, express ourselves about the inexpressible. We do not express the inexpressible; we exemplify it.

viii

Talking to oneself and talking to Brahman are two different things. Listening to Brahman and listening to oneself are the same thing.

ix

The dog's bark goes through the silence, and the silence gives thanks, for now it knows what it is not. Blessed is the Great Silence in the market place. It is what all the barking is about. Everyone is bargaining for silence at the top of his lungs.

It is not necessary for everyone to be silent. If they were, it would be necessary to bark.

x

The Search is not a getting but a granting. . . . Valuable man, thou art infinitely desired: Offer thyself!

xi

The true asking and the true granting are the same act.

xii

Of all the things I have read, I understand only what I have written. Of the things I have written, I understand only what might have been written by anyone.

xiii

I have less to say than ever before. That is because everything is said in a word. Anything less than the whole requires libraries.

xiv

Write any time, say anything, one can never get it all said—so one thinks. Actually, one can sandwich everything between two lines—as if the two lines did not exist.

❖❖❖❖❖❖❖❖❖ *The Key Cage*

i

How can a ghost communicate? Not by Science or Common Sense or the other modalities of the Trance. He cannot lay hands on you or trip you or pry you into the abyss with a syllogism. Perhaps frighten you by simply standing before you?—perhaps confuse you into tripping yourself? But it is all trickery. You will always be able to refute him by a logical denial of the evidence of your senses, or by a sensuous denial of logic, or by the statement that you are mad and given to hallucinations. But even in the depths of your madness, you are responsible and accountable to that naked spirit from which you have fled.

ii

You see how it is. The reply to analysis can only be figurative, because that is the closest approximation to the Language of Events, which is the object of analysis.

For the moment let us be logical, since we bring to logic the acknowledgment of forms, their error or fitness according to contradiction or noncontradiction—though God alone knows what substance we bring to them.

Logic is our attempt to come to agreement with each other upon that which has already eternally and substantially agreed upon us.

That is to say, logic is self-contained, and does not contain self. Or one might say—The birds that blossom on the wire are representing what they mean.

iii

Now that I am ruined, let us speak of naked things. The *prose* does not matter. Do not think to test It by Logic or Good Taste or by Common Sense or by Science, for these are not absolute. You can only test it or not test it by that uncreated essence of yourself which is Brahman.

iv

And do you ask who the Speaker is? First of all, you must ask yourself the question: Who am I?

Then you will prefer that the Speaker remain anonymous, as he essentially is.

v

If you argue with me, let us take extreme positions without further waste of time. With a little practice we can set up a real opposition in a few sentences, and there we have the antinomy for today. Each of us recognizes the equal truth of the other's position. Then, both of us talking harmoniously at the same time, we form a single element in a larger controversy with two other people. The process is repeated, until Mankind addresses Brahman in an attempt to involve him in the argument. He does not reply, because he is all original utterance, that is, Being—upon which the argument is centered. Since he does not reply in terms of the argument, we speak for him. If we did not, we could never succeed in telling ourselves whether we were correct or not—and man has always insisted on grading his own papers. This is very serious make-believe, for civilization is based upon it, and indeed Brahman actually manifests himself to us in this very make-believe, though not necessarily as we wish.

Our continual attempts to be aware of this basic fact become distractions. Culture is an accumulation of reminders, whose obverse is distraction.

vi

The world wills a spirit that passes through walls. The spirit wills a world that passes through thought. The world thereby confesses that its walls are not what they seem, and the spirit confesses that its thought has neither form nor content outside the Object that occupies it. But the Reality is only completed when, after the mutual exposé, the opposites confess themselves to one another in the harmony and simplicity which have really been prevailing all along.

vii

Theology is largely the result of a misunderstanding. But it is impossible to evade Brahman by misunderstanding. Every response we make to his utterances is ambiguous, and every alternative we suggest is full of silence and Brahman: full of silence signifying that we do understand, full of Brahman because he will not abandon us and we will not abandon him even in our most effective apostasy, the loss of creative consciousness that is characterized by a radical indifference.

viii

You do not understand? You wish to be enlightened? One must be enlightened already to wish such a thing. You will never understand more than you understand at this instant. In dwelling upon reincarnation you are trying to postpone the accounting, as if all incarnations were not possible to you at this instant—all alternatives, all interpretations, all evasions, the least effective of which is to be—or to pretend to be—an ignoramus.

With every beat of your heart, with every breath you draw, you are wholly present, total, and fulfilled, and the well-timed measure of your organism is here and now, here and now complete, replete, crossed by eternity.

ix

The philosopher is a craftsman. His constant handling of ideas with his head (as Ram the blacksmith handles pots with his toes) makes him prone to an occupational disease, the Reasoning Madness. This refers to the passion of reason, which its victims hold to be the only real passion.

Philosopher, subjective passions vibrate in every objective word you utter; your anguished heart howls out of your objective sentences. Philosopher, how can you endure it!

Any child can recognize the pride without being able to follow the dialectic. And the child is right in believing the pride to be the decisive factor. It is hard to fool a child, impossible to fool the nature of things.

You make off with the word "subjectivity"? You are welcome to it. Nothing is changed. Make off with all words if you like. You have already done so in your haste. Everything is changed, of course, but it would be changed in any case. Like Potiphar's wife, you are left with an empty coat, and the ineluctable content of Reality flees from you, afflicted as you are with logorrhea!

x

But to attack philosophy is precisely as foolish as to defend it. The wise man is totally responsive to persons, including their universal setting, and the dialectic practiced by them (and by himself) is as dear to him as any other universalizing motion. But he refuses absolutely to confine his responsiveness to the terms of any particular mode of communication.

The wise man appreciates foolishness just as much as he appreciates wisdom. He appreciates everything, even philosophy. Of course, any motion that leads to the baffling, the bankrupting, and the breaking of the individual ego may be a step toward wisdom. . . . Any sickness will do.

xi

Objective results are never decisive; nevertheless the subjective apologist is driven to crafty and disingenuous methods disguised as logical progression. There is no objective solution short of the logical cessation of logic, which is the inherent necessity of logical progression if the act of cessation is not to remain a challenge to logic. But we must act as if this were not the case, in order not to divest ourselves of objective language with which we attempt to make love sound plausible. And of course love is anything but plausible.

Love is an absurdity to logic because it is the key to the logician's cage.

xii

And yet love is never difficult. When we think it is, we are loving ourselves too passionately.

xiii

"Thou shalt love thy neighbor as thyself."

But if I love, he is not he, I am not I. I have no neighbor.

"Love one another."

But there is no other.

"Love One, then."

But there is not One, because that is to oppose to it me and you—the One and the Many.

"Love, then."

That is to suppose that there is another possibility for Being.

"Be!"

Yes, it is only possible for Being to be. It is not possible for Being not to be. It is not possible for Not-Being to be or not to be.

xiv

When I saw Jean Cocteau's great film masterpiece *The Blood of a Poet,* it occurred to me that one should see everything basically three times: as simple man, as fallen man, and as regenerate man. It could all happen at once in the sense that the drama of the individual has no necessary chronological sequence, but is manifested on the principle of simultaneity—that is, the whole of Being is present at every point of time. But the actualizing of pure possibility is a quality of Being expressing itself; so history, or time, or the unfulfilled, is necessary to Being, but chronological sequence is accidental, Hegel to the contrary. At any point Spirit can cut across Process to the Absolute, in the sense that the whole of Process can be manifested as well in an instantaneous vision as in a long history.

Hegel's whole philosophy would have been profoundly affected (perhaps to the point of disappearance) had he studied the Bhagavad Gita or Zen Buddhism or even the Sermon on the Mount on *its* terms.

Nevertheless, I am grateful to those who think Reality. Had they not seen their way clear to creating themselves, we could not have been born even once.

xv

Among the animals there is a law, that each must represent what is meant.

A Visionary Mollusk

i

The Virgin does not think. She said to me: "If you must think, think love. But I would impress on you that there is no translation of Being."

Yes, God is always seeking a place in which to be born of himself.

And all places are seeking to be the place, and in their seeking, God is crossed.

I can only be born of a virgin; and that virgin is myself.

"But I am not a virgin!"

"Try."

ii

It is the function of all symbols to declare their own inadequacy by referring to that which is adequate. They are adequate if they do this.

The greatest symbol is Man himself. In his conscious imperfection he is certain that he is destined to exemplify the perfection of a Reality which can never exhaust him and which he can never exhaust.

Like all symbols, Man must be accepted and he must be rejected—simultaneously.

iii

The isolated intersection of two lines at right angles to each other: that is a cross.

A cross is uncompromisingly direct, wholly devoid of oblique angles, confronting you squarely with nothing else and nothing less than the one center at which two diametrically opposed progressions meet.

This pure, unique directness is an insecurity to the senses upon which aesthetic appreciation depends, for it is neither beautiful nor ugly, but absolute. It is immovable progression, the incomprehensible mystery and factual paradox that constitutes the perfect affront to logic. It is the living, naked, dynamic *crux*, the very thought of which produces discomfort, even to the point of love. Indeed, it is a rude shock; it does violence to all the sinuous ways of human existence itself.

A circle is another matter. Man takes comfort in circles. A circle is the same all over. The world is a circle.

As soon as the circle is thought in relation to a point either inside or outside itself, however, it ceases to be simply a circle, and becomes a circle crossed or a cross circled. (If the circle is thought to have a center, for example, then it ceases to be primarily a circle, and is instead a linear progression between a point and an equidistant periphery beyond which it extends infinitely.)

Move from the circle, and there is a cross. Do not move, and there is a cross. The cross confronts you in every responsible action, and in every irresponsible action. The circle is not primarily, but only incidentally, a circle.

Two opposing progressions are demanded by the cross: that you go to it, and that you leave it—both simultaneously. All your actions must lead to this center, and they must all stem from this center. That is the demand.

This center is the unity of opposites: of the Individual and the Universal, the Will and Destiny, Thought and Reality, Time and

Eternity, Existence and Being. As such, it is the seat of identity.

To be nailed by one's karma upon the absolute center of reality, where alone all the mighty and fateful tides of the universe intersect their opposites; there, amid total agony, to embody the death of the Will-to-Power, of the Idea, of the entire resources of the individual Ego: that is to die the death—that is to be self-crucified.

iv

Man is a visionary mollusk who absorbs certain small particles and secretes meaning. The survival value of this is that it helps him to identify himself with the shoal of mollusks, thereby intensifying his nature—which could as well secrete perfume or some other exciting substance.

v

To survive, we must wrong each other. To thrive, we must love. We should do both of these things with a certain dash, since it is only to ourselves that they can be definitive.

vi

If the Enemy is great, it is because we are on his side.

vii

The one sure thing that comes from the rubbing of elbows is friction. To establish a world government, people will have to recognize the detestability of themselves as well as of all other groups. Groups can never love one another; they can only prevent love. The best they can do is to enforce laws to keep themselves from harming other groups, and other groups from harming them.

Recognizing the evil in all groups, the individual should then practice *universal discrimination;* that is, he should discriminate *absolutely*, not against this or that group, but against all groups. He will discriminate firmly against the human race. He will forgive, but he will not forget the unfortunate antecedents of the few whom he chooses to constitute the motley élite of his spirit.

viii

Man is a minority. . . . Man is a minority of a minority. . . . The closer I get to him, the farther he gets from me. . . . Man does not exist.

How to prove the existence of Man? Scotus Erigena: "Man is a certain intellectual idea formed eternally in the Divine Mind." The same argument by which Anselm of Canterbury proves the existence of God should be used to prove the existence of Man. One says to God, who enjoys playing the Devil's Advocate:

"Thou hast the *idea* of Man in Thy mind, dost Thou not?"

"I do."

"And Thou admittest that the idea is that of a being than whom nothing greater can be conceived to exist?"

"Certainly." (Had He objected, the entire structure of the universe would have crumbled, to re-form again only after many Kalpas.)

"Then, since reality is greater than the idea of it, this being can only be conceived to exist in reality?"

"This," says God, "will require thought, whereas I am Infinite, Indivisible Subjectivity wrapped in the Cloud of Unknowing. Give Me a little time." And He takes time. But to take time, He must enter time; that is, He must be incarnated again in order to examine the question, Whether Man exists?

A State of Being

i

Though I smoke a great Mohammedan hookah with a hose six feet long and sit in an American armchair and peruse the *Times of India* and rest my feet on a huge dog—I am not solid. If you so much as shift your head a little, my form will flicker and metamorphose into that moth whom you see trying so unsubstantially to possess the source of the light. If you close your eyes I shall become a fantastic process of distraction and rapprochement.

I fly pell-mell through time; I voyage continually like a society of birds. What do you think you are looking at, anyway? You gape as though you thought you saw something.

ii

Thou art our point of continual departure. Thou art unsounded. Look, I am essentially Thee!

iii

"Now that we are alone—"

"We are always alone, little man. Art thou not charmed?"

iv

The hand of the Master does not waver; but the canvas has its own will: it may receive the Image fully or it may remain mere canvas—a masterpiece or a nonentity.

v

The next best thing to seeing is reading about seeing. The next best thing to Being is Not-Being.

The decision to abandon Culture for Being is the last act of Culture.

When one is grounded in Being, one may read books once again, but the act, the reader, and that which is read are not the same as before.

The carpenter saws off wood. Then he saws off the deceptive years. Then he saws off his self. Then he does not know what he is doing, but he knows that he does not. So he saws off wood as before. It is not the same carpenter, not the same act, not the same wood; but who can tell the difference?

vi

It is not necessary that you understand me as you wish, but only that you wish to understand me.

vii

If you wish to know me, do not distract yourself with my history. If you wish to know my history, do not distract yourself with me. Here I am—in the source of your desire to know me, infinitely prior to the desire.

But you cannot know the ahistorical except through the discipline of the historical, that is, through the systematic evolution of your failure? In your failure you will know me. In time you will come to admit that you already know me timelessly.

viii

When the features of your individual character are so worn away that they are like those of an ancient, buried statue, then you are general and anonymous, transcending time and place.

The individual will intends ultimately to extend itself until it is so general that it has no limiting opposition, it is coextensive with the sum total of reality, and no name of separate identity can be applied to it. It intends the anonymity of God.

The difference between God's will and Satan's is only a subtle, absolute nuance.

ix

Let us not quibble about a metaphor for the basic continuum of Reality that surrounds and fills us.

To the man who stands belongingly in this continuum, no event that may be predicated of him is inappropriate. All circumstances are just, and all are equally appreciable, as are their opposites, and also his practical partisanship in which he loves his enemies, both those within himself and those without. All are expressions of Reality, and as "mere" expressions, none of them is decisive or adequate to this man's identity. Indeed, nothing may properly be predicated of him, insofar as he is himself, any more than it may be predicated of Brahman. His simple stance in Now forestalls all predicates by being their unutterable source.

He is mysterious because he is real.

x

How hard it is to love when one has other resources, unstable though they are!

xi

We do not wish to be distracted from the central reality, so we select certain parts of existence and exclude them as being especially distracting. The exclusions may be distractions, and we may have to exclude the exclusions. This is to make a quantitative analysis of something that is indifferent to quantity. Actually, we could exclude everything, and still be no closer to the central reality, except in the sense that we should be so alienated from reality that it would be beyond human endurance to sustain the opposition without effecting a reconciliation.

The rapprochement does not depend on the selective arrangement of external situations, but upon a simple, radical shift in being, from which the point of view follows. In terms of the point of view, one shifts from the criteria of selection to the principle of inclusion—or rather one *has* shifted, since the one real selection was the fatal one.

xii

The condition of idealism is a part of reality. So is an unrealistic attitude. Realism is also a part of reality; it sees what is concrete, without confusing it with moral and metaphysical possibilities, even though it is aware of such confusion as a concrete phenomenon. It withdraws its will that reality be other than what it is, because it wills itself, realism, to be real. At this point it becomes radical idealism, resting on the grace of Brahman.

To be real, we must use our imagination.

xiii

So long as I flash, I am at war.

Beyond the Reef

i

Chuang Tzü says, "The real man is absent-minded."

The absent-minded man cannot remember his bad deeds; he cannot remember his good deeds. He forgets to be elated at not remembering the one, and he forgets to be chagrined at not remembering the other. He cannot remember who he is, or *that* he is. He takes everything that is given him and lets it go. He has no roof, no floor, no walls. Infinity finds him irresistible.

ii

I am looking for a book—always. I am never discouraged by the fact that it has not been written and never will be—indeed, this knowledge alone makes my search legitimate.

Wisdom is the name of a long book which would have to be dispensed with if it were written.

iii

Wisdom is the favorite wife of Folly. It is her *dharma* to sit at his feet and to serve him.

iv

How to Settle an Account

The wise man has settled his account—how? By calling the whole thing off. He refuses to prosecute; he refuses to defend.

At any time, having settled his accounts, he is ready to live or to die. It is all equal. The main thing was to settle the account.

v

Nothing stands for itself or is meaningful in itself, but everything is great by virtue of its limitations. Everything is an impresario.

At the limits of each thing there is a hush, in which the stranger is introduced—always under a pseudonym, although his identity is an open secret.

The Journeying Way

i

Nirvana is a habit, is it not? It takes nothing short of a lifetime to acquire it. . . . Indeed, there are those who maintain stoutly that it requires many lifetimes. In any case, short cuts to the present instant are unreliable.

ii

There is a place beyond peace, a place of risk, adventure, action. The way is up and the way is down; it leads through the hungers and the satisfactions of the Buddhist Hell and the Christian Purgatory and the Hindu Nirvana, the blessed abode of peace. What am I saying? That there is a place beyond Nirvana?

This "beyond" has the semblance of everyday existence in the world; but the *life* experienced there is in another modality, because it comes of a deliberate, direct transfer of the personality from Nirvana back to the earthly affairs in which it originated so long ago. It has been called the Incarnation.

In this Place of the Great Return, this Beyond, this *World*, Nirvana is challenged and tested if at any point it prove to be unreal or unfinished.

But the Incarnated One is so almost ordinary because he experiences what all men experience. . . . Who can tell the difference?

I assure you, it is not easy to become ordinary.

187

iii

Amor is that agent in the soul which impels us to return to him. Although we have left him, he has not left us.

Then what have we to do?

The trick is to do nothing.

You need not take one step toward him. You need only to refrain from seeking any more. He has been ready for you all the time, at every instant, but you simply cannot believe in the possibility of an encounter without the most strenuous exertions. And all the time you are breaking your heart and your back to achieve it, he is patiently standing beside you, holding your coat for you.

iv

And this waiting, which is interminable because he has already arrived in the station and we stand, back to back, waiting for one another. . . . Loitering is not forbidden.

But of course waiting is not waiting either. We wait for our own arrival and for his, but we are both already there. Signs all over the place affirm the fact in the principal unspoken languages of the world.

v

Truth is wherever you decide to face it. The seeker wanders. The finder wonders. All travel.

In the seeker you see a man in full flight.

vi

I go into a perilous place. There is but one danger—that I shall not be myself: Not that I may pretend, but that I may not recognize that I am myself, absolutely imperiled and absolutely secure.

vii

It is not necessary to take a formal farewell. Just go. Quietly.
Never mind making up an inventory of the things you are leav-
ing. Just leave them.
"But there are a thousand and one things—"
Goodbye, my friend.

Now the world walks away. I am alone with the world.
First, in the silent world, sitting still, I dine on silence.
Then, in the silent world, am consumed in silence.